Praise for Solving Crim

"EPIC. It's got a fantastic cast of characters and the writing is so funny my jaw hurt from laughing and smiling. Literally. We'll all be talking about this book!"
Rashmi Sirdeshpande, author of *Good News*

"I want more!!! Give me more Lessore!"
Claire Powell, author of *Marty Moose*

"Witty, wacky and full of warmth and humour... bright and bold storytelling."
Davina Tijani, author of *The Nkara Chronicles*

"Joyously silly yet a really touching story about finding your own kind of special."
J. P. Rose, author of *Birdie*

"A brilliantly imaginative adventure."
Sophie Cameron, author of *Away With Words*

"A giggle a minute, with brilliantly rib-tickling illustrations."
Rachel Morrisroe, author of *Supersausage to the Rescue*

"A sharp and sparky adventure packed full of humour and fantastic characters, this series has everything you could want. A delight from start to finish!"
Dave Rudden, author of *Knights of the Borrowed Dark*

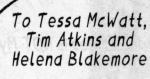

To Tessa McWatt,
Tim Atkins and
Helena Blakemore

– N.L.

To Mum, Ruby
and Stella

– S.S.

LITTLE TIGER

An imprint of Little Tiger Press Limited
1 Coda Studios, 189 Munster Road, London SW6 6AW
www.littletiger.co.uk

Imported into the EEA by Penguin Random House Ireland,
Morrison Chambers, 32 Nassau Street, Dublin D02 YH68
www.littletigerpress.com

A paperback original

First published in Great Britain in 2025
Text copyright © Nathanael Lessore, 2025
Illustration copyright © Simran Singh, 2025

ISBN: 978-1-78895-664-2
ISBN: 978-1-78895-789-2 (Exclusive edition)
e-ISBN: 978-1-78895-774-8

A CIP catalogue record for this book is available from the British Library.

Printed and bound in the UK.
STP/3400/0631/1224

MIX
Paper | Supporting
responsible forestry
FSC® C171272

The Forest Stewardship Council® (FSC®) is a global, not-for-profit organization dedicated to the
promotion of responsible forest management worldwide. FSC® defines standards based on agreed
principles for responsible forest stewardship that are supported by environmental, social, and
economic stakeholders. To learn more, visit www.fsc.org

2 4 6 8 10 9 7 5 3 1

SOLVING CRIMES IS NOT MY SUPERPOWER

NATHANAEL LESSORE

ILLUSTRATED BY

SIMRAN DIAMOND SINGH

LITTLE TIGER

LONDON

IN THE BEGINNING...

In a time before smartphones, when children had only sticks and a rock to play with, when black and white were the only two colours invented, explorer Valkro Strapp settled in the town of Walsham. He brought with him an ancient treasure, found in the mystical caves of Magaluf.

Soon after his arrival eighty years ago, the inhabitants of Walsham started noticing changes. It began with small, magical events, like plants blossoming whenever Ms Dorris walked through

5

her garden, or Mr David's nose growing longer whenever he told the truth. (Or so he said.)

Since the treasure came to town, the sun shone brighter all year round. Walsham was blessed with eternal summer, while the rest of the country stayed as wet and cold as a dog's nose.

More people started noticing that they had extraordinary abilities: some were given the strength to lift mountains, others the power to leap across oceans. Others gained very unextraordinary abilities, like the power to make a cow fall over. Or the power of making sandals and socks look cool. ➔

6

As time passed, most of the inhabitants gradually discovered a unique gift, a power, early on, sometimes as young as nursery age. (These days, the children of Walsham generally develop "super" powers by the time they finish primary school.)

When Valkro took his treasure with him on an exploratory tour of Grimsby, the inhabitants of that town also began showing signs of superpowers. But, from the moment he left Walsham, terrible things started to happen there. (Much more terrifying and dreadful than the invention of Crocs.)

When Valkro Strapp came home, he was devastated to find his beloved town in disarray, but fortunately it didn't take long for Walsham to recover once the intrepid explorer and his treasure had returned. So, he stayed in Walsham.

Weeks turned into months. Months turned into more months and then years.

As Valkro got older, the powerful magic from his treasure protected him like a lucky charm. He never got ill, never ran out of toilet paper, never banged his toe on the table leg, and he was always finding five-pound notes in his back pocket.

Valkro lived to be ninety years old, and on his eighty-ninth birthday he hid his prized possession somewhere in Walsham itself. Somewhere nobody would find it, in the hope that it would never leave town again. It was the only way to keep Walsham safe, sunny and sizzling with superpowers.

And as to the whereabouts of this mysterious treasure? Well, as no one knows what it looks like, it has never been found. Let's hope it stays that way – who knows what would happen if it fell into the wrong hands...?

THURSDAY

JUST BEFORE EVERYTHING WENT **WRONG**

CHAPTER 1

Most towns have a mail person who goes door to door, putting mail through the letter box. It must take ages strolling from one house to another, to another. Then you have to start on a new street and do it all again.

Here in Walsham, the postal worker has **EIGHT ARMS** that stretch as far as he wants. He delivers the post to eight houses at a time, although he doesn't have complete control over all his arms.

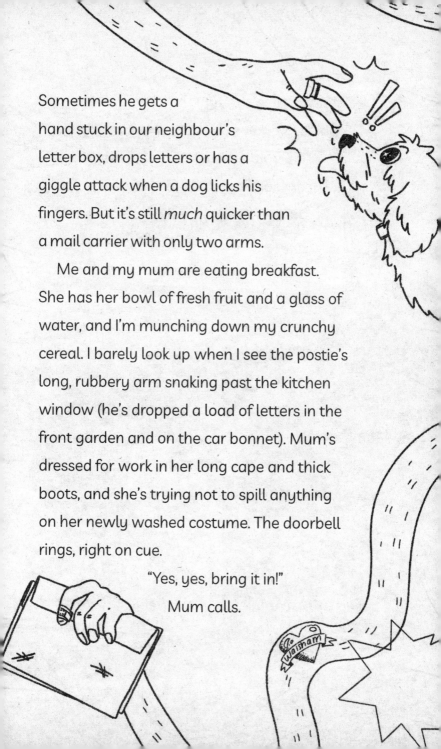

Sometimes he gets a hand stuck in our neighbour's letter box, drops letters or has a giggle attack when a dog licks his fingers. But it's still *much* quicker than a mail carrier with only two arms.

Me and my mum are eating breakfast. She has her bowl of fresh fruit and a glass of water, and I'm munching down my crunchy cereal. I barely look up when I see the postie's long, rubbery arm snaking past the kitchen window (he's dropped a load of letters in the front garden and on the car bonnet). Mum's dressed for work in her long cape and thick boots, and she's trying not to spill anything on her newly washed costume. The doorbell rings, right on cue.

"Yes, yes, bring it in!"

Mum calls.

After wiggling through the letter box, the postal worker's stretchy arm, carrying a shiny gold envelope, weaves along the corridor. His hand feels its way round the kitchen door and hovers towards Mum. He accidentally **PRODS** her face with the envelope a few times before she manages to grab it.

"Yes, thank you, Gary!" she says.

The hand gives her a thumbs up, before snaking back to the front door, knocking over a milk carton on the way out.

Mum tears open the gold envelope and reads her IPA missions for the day. I roll my eyes as she pushes her empty bowl away. She stands up slowly, hands on hips, chest out, in her **SIGNATURE SUPERHERO POSE**.

"Mum, you're doing it again," I tell her.

Mum clocks how she's standing and straightens up. "Oh, sorry, Sara! I don't even realise I'm doing it." She comes round and gives me a kiss on the top of my head.

Mum and Dad are part of the **IPA** (Incredible Protection Agency), so they're basically superheroes for the whole country. People from other areas tried moving to Walsham to get powers, but the town wasn't big enough. Part of the IPA agreement is that our heroes **FIGHT CRIME** everywhere, so other places let us be.

Only people with helpful superpowers can

join the IPA, as long as they're brave enough.
Mum can **CONTROL THE WIND** – she uses it to
fly around and put out forest fires.
She's great for flying kites but not
so great around birthday candles.
Dad has **SUPER STRENGTH** – his
leg muscles mean he can jump
from here to the next
village in just one leap.
Even though criminals
are terrified of him, really he is
a big, soft teddy bear. He once
slammed on the brakes of the
car, nearly causing a major
accident, when a butterfly
flew across the road.

"Where is your father?" Mum says,
checking her watch. His hot oats and protein bars
are untouched in front of his chair.

"I think he's having trouble with his **NEMESIS**,"
I say.

She purses her lips and we both shake our heads. The problem with being part of the IPA is that every superhero needs a nemesis.

Dad's used to be some villain called **CHESTNUT THE CONKERER**, but after the IPA defeated him, he turned his life around and got heavily into pottery. I think Dad became bored without having a villain to beef with, and then **THE WARDEN** showed up. He's our local traffic warden and his name is Norman – he's actually very friendly. He gave my dad a ticket once, and Dad started rolling around on the floor, screaming, "Nooooo!" and crying in pain. They've been **MORTAL ENEMIES** since that fateful day. Shout out Norman.

"You want a lift to school?" Mum asks.

"No, thanks. It's a nice day as usual – I'm just gonna walk it."

I hate it when she "gives me a lift". She legit carries me in her arms as we fly over the town. It's so embarrassing. I usually ask her to land behind a tree at the end of the road and put me down where the other kids won't see.

On the way out of the house, Dad is losing it because of another parking ticket. Norman is nowhere to be seen but Dad is on one knee, wailing, with his arms outstretched.

BY THE STRENGTH OF POSEIDON, BY THE BRAIDS OF BOB MARLEY, BY THE BICYCLES IN BEIJING, I WILL VANQUISH THESE FOES AND SAIL INTO THE SUNSET OF VICTORY!

Sometimes my dad can be a little dramatic. Mum says he's just sensitive.

"Bye, Dad!" I call out.

He puts his arms down and stops screaming to say, "Bye, munchkin. Have a great day at school. And remember: the only **TRUE** powers are..."

"...a loving heart, a helping hand and the courage to do what's right."

He says that every day. It used to be cool but now it just feels a bit cringey.

You see, I don't actually have a superpower. Which is odd for a ten-year-old who lives in Walsham. I'm already in the last few weeks of Year Five, and pretty much everyone in my class at Walsham Primary has already discovered theirs. I'm sure they all think there's something wrong with me and I don't blame them. It's weird.

I'm trying to do little things to discover what my gift is. I thought it might be cooking but I can't even make cereal without burning it. Maybe burning cornflakes is my power? No, Sara, that's silly. Maybe it's **SILLINESS**! I puff my cheeks out and tickle myself under the chin like a goat.

"Sara, are you OK? Why are you doing that to your face?" Mum calls out of the window.

DEFINITELY silly but **NOT** super...

"I was just checking something!" I call back.

OK, silliness is not my superpower. Even though I do feel rather silly right now.

On the way to school, I pass by the nail salon and see Yasmine inside. She has the power to see **VISIONS OF THE PAST**. (It's cool because she never has to google anything.)

Our mayor has **MULTICOLOURED FARTS**. Seriously, a puff of colourful smoke appears every time he lets one rip.

Hey, I didn't say they were all amazing powers! Most people have pretty pointless ones. I know an old lady who can **LEVITATE SQUIRRELS** – only waist-high – and she loves going to the park to feed them. Her husband's power is **COOKING PASTA IN HIS MOUTH**. Mum doesn't enjoy going to theirs for dinner.

But why???

Georgie and Javier are already waiting by the school gates. Georgie is wearing her full football kit and doing kick-ups. She's way more athletic than I am. Georgie can do all the tricks – round-the-world, flick-ups, balancing the ball on her head, and that's not even her superpower. Georgie's special ability is that she can **SMELL FEAR**. Oh, and she's my best friend in the whole world. She's brave and funny, and extremely loyal. Georgie's been there for me since our first day of school.

Just in case it wasn't clear, Georgie lives and breathes football. Her parents are both football managers. They don't say goodbye in the morning, they just shake hands and shout, "Good game out there," and when she got chickenpox in Reception they blamed the ref.

And then there's Javier. He's good at spelling. I think that's his superpower?

"That's not my power," Javier says, and I realise I've been thinking out loud. He puffs out his chest slightly. **"MY POWER IS—"**

"Javier, don't be insensitive." Georgie cuts him off quickly.

"Right. Sorry, Sara," he mumbles sheepishly, looking down at the ground. It's so annoying that everyone has a special gift except me. I've always wanted a cool power, something that would get me into the IPA like my parents.

Sometimes I dream of having my own nemesis. Not Norman the traffic warden (he's too nice) but maybe someone like Margaret Chow, who's the class know-it-all and one of the popular girls in our year. Her special gift is **SENSING DOGS' EMOTIONS**, which is not exactly nemesis-worthy. But it's still a power.

I groan out loud.

"Your time will come." Georgie puts her arm round my shoulder as we walk through the school gates.

"Jeez, I hope you're right."

At this point, I'd settle for something less cool, like the janitor who can draw **PERFECT CIRCLES**, or Judy in the year above us who has **MUSICAL HICCUPS**.

"And besides, powers or no powers, we think you're a **COMPLETE BOSS**."

Javier nods in agreement.

"Thanks, guys." They always have my back.

I have their backs too, for example, by helping in

history, which is our first lesson of the day.

"Do you think Henry the Eighth and Henry the Hoover were related?" Georgie asks as we head to class.

"No," I reply. "I do not."

"But they're both called Henry. And they both have 'the' as their middle name," she says.

Javier starts nodding, then looks at me and starts shaking his head.

"Oh, Georgie..." How do I put this? "You're a genius when it comes to football," I finish.

"Thanks." She smiles. "That reminds me: the final is only four days away," she says, clapping her hands excitedly. "We're gonna smash Ramsdale to smithereens! They won't know what hit 'em."

Me and Javier grin at each other. Ramsdale is the only other school in Walsham. Even though the kids there have powers too, we never lose to them. Georgie only mentions the final, like, every day but her excitement levels are infectious. I don't

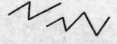

22

play football but even I'm excited about it.

"What makes you so sure it'll be that easy?" Javier asks, before blushing bright red like a sun-dried tomato. He's different to the kids in our class, but in a good way. Georgie once made him laugh so hard a baked bean shot out of his nose and straight into his shirt pocket. He's been hanging with us ever since.

"Oh, I didn't say it would be easy!" Georgie shakes her head. "I just said we're gonna smash 'em."

We all duck out of the way to avoid two students **FLOATING** along the corridor ceiling.

Georgie continues. "Walsham Primary hasn't lost a game in years, not since that mysterious trophy turned up."

Javier rolls his eyes and I smile. She's been obsessed with this idea since we were in Reception.

"As long as we've got that trophy, we can—" She stops in her tracks and gasps.

The trophy cabinet has been broken in to: there are bits of glass everywhere.

Only one trophy has been taken. But it's the most important one.

CHAPTER 2

Students are milling around in the hallway, muttering.

Did you see it?

Why would anyone steal it?

Crowds are fun – let's join in and whisper stuff.

The school football cup has been there since **_FOREVER_**.

"No, no, no, no," Georgie moans. "Our cup final is in four days and I'm the captain. I'm telling you, guys, that trophy's more than a trophy – it's our **_GOOD-LUCK_** charm. We need it back!"

She's looking around, as if the thief could pop up any minute, but all we can see are worried faces. Poor Georgie.

"*I need it back.*" There are tears in her eyes. This is really important to her.

I don't care about superstitions but I do care that my best friend is upset. Why would some thief decide to break in to the cabinet four days before the final and steal the only trophy that she cares about?

I clench my fists. Nobody messes with my friends.

"What are we going to do?" Georgie sobs.

"We're going to get you that trophy back – I promise."

26

It's too loud out here. The Year Four with **FIREWORK HANDS** are 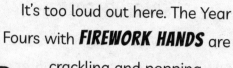 crackling and popping behind me. And some kid keeps running round the cabinet, screaming, "**THE END IS NIGH!**"

I turn to Georgie. "We need to go come up with a plan." Then I look at Javier. "You in?"

"Always," he says.

I put my thumb under my chin, our secret sign that I'm proud of him. He does it back.

Cool. I close my eyes and start mapping out our next move.

Trophy missing. Georgie sad.

"We should investigate the **CRIME SCENE**," I tell them.

The crowd has started to disperse, and it won't be very long until a janitor or someone comes to clean up. I pull out my notepad and flip it open. Javier pulls out his favourite notebook that has a glittery **SPACE-UNICORN** on the cover. He notices me eyeing it up.

"What? I'm not obsessed with it or anything." He goes bright red again.

"I didn't say you were." (I'm not even gonna mention the fact I caught him winking at it once.)

"Why would a unicorn be in space anyway?" Georgie asks. "Didn't they go extinct years ago?"

"No," I say. "They did not. And neither did dragons, mermaids, sausage dogs or the Wakandans."

I can't believe we're having this discussion again! Javier goes to say something else, but I cut him off. We're wasting time. "Guys, let's just focus on the crime scene?"

Georgie sits on the floor, still in shock, but Javier and I take a closer look at what's left...

Nothing. I lean in and take a closer look at what's left of the cabinet. *Hmmm.* It's very dusty but there are no footprints or fingerprints. The thief must've used their powers. Javier notes this down.

That's funny: if I concentrate on the door
frame of the cabinet, it almost looks as if it was
smashed from the inside. Who could be small
enough to climb in *and* big enough to break out?
We're gonna need more information.

"Georgie, what exactly does the trophy look
like? I've never seen it up close."

Now that I'm rummaging through the

wreckage, I realise I've never paid much attention to this cabinet.

"I haven't either," adds Javier.

"Yeah, me neither," Georgie says. We both stop and look at her. "What? It's always been covered in so much dust, I don't even know what colour it is."

Cool. We're searching for something, and we don't really know what it looks like. Hopefully it really is a **LUCKY TROPHY** – that would help a lot.

Either way, there's no signs of human tampering. It's almost as if the trophy was stolen by a ghost. I don't think anyone in Walsham has **GHOST POWERS**. Maybe I could ask my parents. Better yet, I could get them to solve the case.

Ah no, I can't. Mum's saving a bunch of climbers trapped up a cliff, and Dad is carrying a broken-down train back to the station.

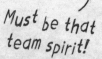

Must be that team spirit!

"Maybe we should let the teachers sort it out. Surely they'll find it before the **FOOTBALL GAME**?" Javier asks timidly.

I shake my head. "Nope, there's no way we're just gonna do nothing."

"Thanks, Sara." Georgie sniffles, shooting Javier a tiny side-eye.

If the teachers don't get the trophy back in time, then we'll just have been sitting around for no reason. That would make me feel so guilty. And, besides, it could have been a teacher that took it in the first place.

We get to our history class early and thankfully the room's empty. We take a seat in the corner at the back. The minute I sit down, my mind goes into **OVERDRIVE** about the missing trophy. I close my eyes again.

OK, think, think.

My parents are superheroes. I'm not.

But maybe I could be.

What if this is it? What if this is how I get my powers? If I lead this little investigation and find the culprit, I'd be helping Georgie, and maybe my abilities will appear. What if my special gift is **SOLVING MYSTERIES**? I could discover who my nemesis is and become the youngest member of the **IPA**. I've seen my parents solve countless crimes – I'm sure I can do it.

I open my eyes. "The game is afoot."

"So, if we find the foot, we'll find whoever stole the trophy?" Georgie says while we wait for our lesson to begin.

Margaret Chow has arrived so we have to lower our voices. She keeps looking round at us suspiciously and shaking her head.

"*What?* No, forget the foot."

I start again, explaining to Georgie and Javier that it's up to us to track down the **CULPRIT** and that we can do this.

I'm rubbing my hands together. Oh, this is exciting! We'll start by finding out more about the missing trophy. My parents always say that there's a **FORMULA** to solving crimes. If you know everything about the "what", "how" and "why", you can always find the "who". I pull out my notebook again and start tapping my pen against my chin.

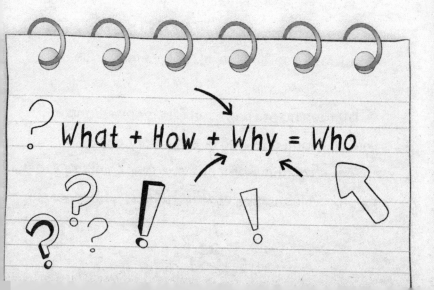

What + How + Why = Who

If we're gonna carry out this investigation, we have to do it properly. We need all the resources available. Books, computers in the IT room, a list of potential **SUSPECTS**, the lot. I picture the broken cabinet in my mind.

"The only trophy that was stolen was the 'lucky' one." I'm thinking out loud. "It can't be a teacher – they don't have anything to gain from us losing a football final."

"Someone from a different school?" Javier suggests.

"Maybe. That does seem more likely," I tell him. Javier smiles to himself.

Georgie mentions her **NEMESIS** – the captain of Ramsdale's football team. That seems possible.

Think, Sara, think.

I'm tapping my pen even faster now. "So, it must be someone who doesn't want our team to win. It could be someone else who thinks the trophy is blessed with **GOOD LUCK**, or someone with a **VENDETTA** against Georgie. I guess that narrows it down."

Now that we have some potential "*whos*", we need to investigate the "*what*" to work out who is the "*who*" that did it. We must learn as much about the trophy as possible. We should go to the IT room as soon as we can.

I look at Georgie, bravely holding back her tears. I look at Javier, his lip quivering. I know the last thing he wants to do is go chasing after an actual criminal. But the **COURAGE** to do what's right trumps all that fear.

"Guys. Let's go catch a criminal."

Our lesson has started, and Miss Teree is explaining all about the town hero's missing treasure. We've already heard it a **THOUSAND** times so only Margaret Chow and her gaggle of friends are sitting upright and taking notes, glowering at the rest of the class. Amelia and Evie are playing rock-paper-scissors under the desk, their hands literally **TRANSFORMING** into a rock, a sheet of paper or a pair of scissors.

"We know that Valkro Strapp's hidden treasure is what gives the townsfolk their special abilities,"

Miss Teree tells us. She demonstrates by sticking out her tongue and a **SPARKLY RAINBOW** falls out of her mouth. "Not, as someone suggested last week, a high-fibre diet and a can-do attitude."

Georgie blushes and sinks down in her chair. Margaret Chow turns to smirk.

I stick my tongue out at her, then wonder if I have similar powers to Miss Teree. I open my mouth wide and say,

"**Ahhhhhhhhhhhh.**"

Everyone turns to look at me. "Is everything OK there, Sara?" Miss Teree asks.

"Yep. I was just practising for my dentist's appointment." *Yikes. Good save.*

"As I was saying," she carries on, "eighty years have passed, and the treasure has still not been found. It turns out Mr Strapp was very good at hiding things. We don't know what the treasure looks like but we do know it's somewhere in Walsham because we still have our powers."

Javier raises his hand to ask a question. "Miss, what happens when other people visit Walsham? Do they get powers?"

Before the teacher can answer, Margaret Chow jumps in. "Only people born in Walsham have powers. Isn't that right, miss?"

"Yes, that's right," Miss Teree replies. Margaret sits back smugly in her seat and looks round at me. "What about Sara? She was born here, and she hasn't got any abilities."

I feel my face flush as her wannabes sit there grinning. I glare at her, and Miss Teree

sooooooo smug

tells us to settle down.

"Well, Margaret, some people's abilities can take a little longer to manifest than others. The students in our class without powers just need to stay patient."

She gives me and Javier an encouraging smile. He seems baffled and looks around to see if she's talking to someone else.

"Wait, I do have a power," Javier says. "My power is that I can—" But the school bell cuts him off and drowns out what he was saying.

Everyone starts putting their books away. Out of the corner of my eye I spot Margaret Chow racing out of the classroom before anyone else, even leaving her group of friends behind. *Hmmm, interesting.* Where is she rushing off to?

She always stays behind after lessons. She says, "Classrooms and learning are more fun than fun itself."

I *strongly* disagree. That's like saying, "Carrots are tastier than taste itself."

That's two strange things today – someone stole Georgie's lucky trophy and then Margaret Chow was the first person to leave class. Could they be connected?

???

We're sitting in the canteen, and the food today is terrible. Usually, we have Sunday roast on Thursdays (then sundaes on Mondays and fries on Tuesdays) but today they're serving boiled Brussels sprouts, which smell like a camel sneezed on a dog's bed. We should be eating golden roast potatoes and delicious gravy, but it seems the school cook has forgotten how to make a roast. It's a bit sus but we don't have time to worry about that.

YUCK

"OK, guys, I'm up for suggestions," I say, getting out my notebook.

Javier takes his out too. He blows a kiss to the space-unicorn and, when I catch him, he pretends to do it out of the window instead. Some baffled kid makes eye contact with him and awkwardly waves at us. Georgie waves back.

"We need a list of suspects to investigate," I tell them. "Even if we don't have a gate to invest in."

I start laughing because that joke was pure fire. The others just shrug at each other. I don't care – I'm writing it down. If hilarious jokes are my special ability, I can't deprive the world of that.

"We should add Ramsdale's football captain to the list. Her name's Lilly Padd," Georgie says, thinking out loud. "She's my nemesis. She *knows* how important the trophy is to me."

We all agree.

On to the next suspect.

"Margaret Chow's not very nice to us. Do you think she could be mean enough to steal Georgie's lucky charm?" asks Javier thoughtfully.

"Definitely agree." I add her name.

Suspects List

Lilly Padd
Margaret Chow

That's a good start. Tomorrow we'll begin researching the trophy, build up a list of **CLUES**.

"We need ideas for how to interview the suspects," I tell the others. I'm talking very quietly now because Margaret just sat down behind Javier, and I can tell she's trying to eavesdrop.

But Javier's not even paying attention.

"Javier, will you concentrate? What are you staring at?"

He gulps and points out of the window. There's something in the big blue sky. It's small but it's definitely there.

"It looks like porridge-flavoured candyfloss," I gasp.

"No, it clearly looks like a sheep with

no legs," Margaret corrects me. (I knew she was eavesdropping.)

I roll my eyes. Whatever it *looks* like, it shouldn't be there.

"I think... I think it's a cloud," Javier says.

A ≥**CLOUD**≤ in the sky.

Why is there a cloud in the sky?

We're all staring at it with our mouths wide open. None of us have ever seen a cloud before. How is it so grey and fluffy?

That's yet another strange thing that's happened today. There *must* be a link.

Margaret Chow's friends join her, and now that she's distracted I can lean in to talk to the others. "Guys, does anyone think it's strange that the minute our lucky trophy goes missing, a cloud appears in Walsham?" I ask in a hushed voice.

"Yes," Javier replies, biting his lip.

"I think we need to hurry up and find our thief..."

I'm starting to think that Georgie might *actually* be right about the trophy being lucky.

FRIDAY

AKA FRIYAY BECAUSE WE SAY "YAY" ON FRIDAYS.

WE ALSO SAY LOTS OF OTHER WORDS.

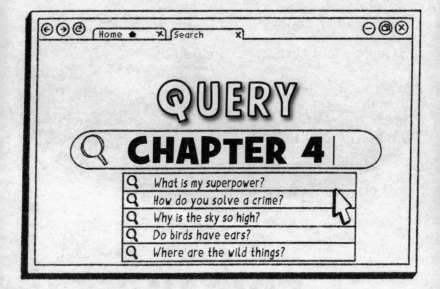

QUERY

CHAPTER 4

- Q What is my superpower?
- Q How do you solve a crime?
- Q Why is the sky so high?
- Q Do birds have ears?
- Q Where are the wild things?

I wake up on Friday ready to eat cereal and **SOLVE CRIMES**. And we're all outta cereal. I'll add it to the shopping list on the fridge. Today we're heading to the IT room to research the trophy.

Last night I told my parents about the investigation and asked their advice. Dad said, "The real crime is that there weren't any snacks or refreshments at your last parents' evening."

Mum said, "You got this, poppet – we believe in you." That was more helpful.

Georgie and Javier are already by the school

gates when I arrive. Javier seems fine, but Georgie looks like she's barely slept.

"You OK?" I ask.

"Not really," she mumbles. "I had a terrible nightmare last night."

"About the trophy?"

"That's how it started but then it got worse and worse." She shudders. "It was terrifying... I was ... playing **CRICKET**." (A boring sport that goes on for days and days – that's Georgie's *worst* nightmare.)

"Let's go find you that trophy," I tell her.

The IT room (also known as Kay's territory) is on the third floor. The lights in the corridor outside are flickering on and off, and there's a strange buzz as we get closer to the door.

"Erm, can anyone else hear bees?" Javier asks.

"How can bees make such a loud buzzing sound when their mouths are so small?" Georgie asks.

Javier thinks about it. "Because there's usually lots of bees making the same noise," he tells her.

"Guys, they make that sound with their wings.

And it's not bees, it's an electrical current. Now can we focus and stop talking about bees?"

The IT department puts me on edge. It's run by Kay Lectron, who has the ability to control **ELECTRICITY**.

"And, besides, we need to ... bee on guard." I giggle at that amazing joke but the others are silent. They must be even more nervous than me. "Un-bee-lievable."

OK, **JOKES** could definitely be my **SUPERPOWER**. That one was hilarious!

I knock on the door and wait for a response.

"Yes?" Kay answers. Their eyes are electric blue and their hair stands upright on their head like they've just put their hands in a plug socket. Even Kay's voice is a little crackly, like it's coming through a walkie-talkie.

"We need to make use of your facilities. Official school business," I tell them. "Please," I add. You have to be polite to Kay: the Wi-Fi at school is at full bars whenever they're happy.

"Request granted," Kay says.

The door swings open. Inside, there are huge screens everywhere. Two rows of students in dark turtlenecks sit there, working away, all sporting headsets. The monitors seem to be tracking some kind of rocket system, and tiny blue sparks **CRACKLE** from Kay's finger when they point at one.

"Keep an eye on that electrical circuit in engine five," Kay says. "And get those satellites into formation." They turn to us. "We're spelling **F*A*R*T** over the moon."

They show us to a little corner of the room for us to do our research. Georgie waves hi as we pass Cami and Jock – they're from her football team. Margaret Chow is also in the corner by herself with a pair of headphones plugged in. I feel my fists clench but I relax them immediately. Mum always tells me that anger is like a wet towel. It's completely useless, and the longer you hold on to it, the heavier it gets.

As we sit down, Kay turns on our screen by blinking at it. Such a flex.

"What exactly are we looking for?" Georgie asks.

I lean forward in my chair and open the browser. "We need to find a picture of the trophy up close."

We find photos of trophies and medals for different sports day events. While I scroll through images, Georgie is shaking with excitement. She bites her lip as we get to a photo that shows a trophy in a cabinet in a very familiar hallway...

"That's it!" Georgie sits bolt upright. Javier shuffles forward in his chair.

"And there's a caption," I tell them as I zoom in. "Trophy mysteriously appears in Walsham school," I read out loud.

Soy de las cuevas, te regalo poderes pero no me muevas...

There are other images that show a guy holding the trophy. He's too pixelated to make out though. The photos are really old – they're dated eighty years ago. The only thing we can see clearly is a moustache. Thank goodness the trophy is clearer.

We start clapping our hands excitedly. I think this is it. Scrolling through, there's a photo of the guy sitting on a see-saw with the trophy on the other end. Then there's one of him and the trophy sharing a milkshake. And another where he's gazing at the trophy over a candlelit dinner.

"Now that we've found some decent pictures, we can start printing posters. If we hang them up around town, maybe someone will have seen it and they can contact us," I tell my friends.

"We did that when my cat went missing," says Georgie.

"Sweet. Did you find the cat?" I ask her.

"No, Mittens went to live on a farm. Then she got run over by a tractor, I think," Georgie replies with a slight frown.

I go to print off the photos when I notice small writing along the front of the trophy.

Soy de las cuevas,
te regalo poderes
pero no me muevas...

I have no idea what that means. It's in another language.

"I'm from the caves, I gift you powers, but don't move me..." Javier says slowly. "It's Spanish."

Caves... Why does that ring a bell? I close my eyes and think back.

Think.

Think.

I'm trying to figure out what it all means while Georgie's still looking at Javier in shock.

53

"Is that your superpower? **SPEAKING SPANISH**?" she asks.

"No." He looks at her blankly. "My family is from Spain. We speak Spanish."

"Right. Yeah." She blushes. "What *is* your power then?"

He opens his mouth to respond but there's a loud **CRACKLING** sound.

The screen goes black. We all gasp. *No!*

The monitors turn off. Every. Single. One. Around us, people are groaning and panicking that they haven't saved their work. Margaret Chow is desperately pressing the power button on her monitor, and someone in the corner screams, "**THE END IS NIGH!**"

I look across the room, over the chaos. Everyone's waving their arms around frantically. There's only one person with the ability to turn off several machines in the blink of an eye.

Kay.

It's no accident that we were *this close* to making a breakthrough in our case and then the power was cut off.

I march straight up to them. "Hey, why did you turn off all the machines?" I huff.

Kay's jaw clenches. I don't think they're used to being challenged in their own domain. "And what if I told you I just felt like it? I don't have to answer to you." Their fingers start crackling with blue sparks the angrier they get.

"Well, you're messing with our investigation, and that's not cool." I don't back down.

But neither does Kay. "I've seen the digital footprints of everyone in this school. I know *everything* about you and your little friends." They glare at me, looking properly menacing. Their whole head is **FIZZING** with electricity.

Georgie and Javier noticed me challenging Kay, so they come over to drag me away. As someone without any powers, Kay could definitely fry me like an onion ring.

"I think you should leave." They scowl.
"In fact," Kay angrily calls out to the rest of
the room, "I think you all should leave!"

Everyone grumbles as they stand up, putting
their things away. One of the kids wearing a
headset and a turtleneck tries to stand up, but
Kay puts their hand on his shoulder. "No, not you,
nameless minion," they tell him.

"Come on, Sara." Javier pulls me by the sleeve. We start heading back to the desk to get our stuff when I notice he's going the long way round.

"You good?" I ask as he rejoins us.

Javier nods, biting his lip. His eyes dart left and right as he folds up a picture of the trophy. It must have printed just before Kay turned the machines off. I breathe a sigh of relief: at least our time here wasn't completely wasted.

"Great job, Javier," I whisper. We quickly put our thumbs under our chins. "There's a photocopier in Miss Teree's classroom. She let me use it once. I'm sure she won't mind."

"Guys, I think we should leave." Georgie is sniffing the air. I recognise that look. She can smell fear.

"Are you sure it's not just Javier?" I ask.

"I don't think so. Javier always smells of fear, but his is like a low, constant smell. This one's different. It's coming from somewhere else in the room."

FEAR

57

"*Gracias*," he says.

"No, it's not grass either," she replies.

Georgie looks around, desperately smelling the air like a mole coming out of hiding. "There are too many people in here. I can't concentrate on who it is."

I look back over at Kay and their electric-blue eyes.

It isn't safe to do our research in here any more, not with Kay controlling all the monitors. I think we have a new suspect, and who knows what they might do next...

CHAPTER 5

We're sitting on our favourite bench in the corner of the playground. More clouds have appeared in the sky, dotted about like spots on a hundred and one Dalmatians. It's so weird seeing these grey blobs. It almost feels like the clouds are spying on us.

Javier's still trembling from the heated exchange with Kay. The way they disrupted our research like that, their behaviour was ... shocking.

Heh, **SHOCKING** – 9/10 joke, Sara. I add more details and a third name to my Suspects List.

* Lilly Padd – Ramsdale football captain with motive to <u>sabotage</u> our team, Georgie's nemesis.

* Margaret Chow – seems to hate us for some reason, especially <u>mean</u> to Georgie.

* Kay Lectron – has read our <u>student files</u>. Possibly knows about Georgie's obsession with the trophy?

"OK, guys." I look up from my notes. "We have suspects. We should have posters that we can hang up in town tomorrow. What else do we need?" Georgie puts her hand in the air. "You don't need to raise your hand. This is a normal conversation." I smile at her.

"Well, as human beings, we need food and oxygen to live." She nods to herself.

I take back what I said about this being a

normal conversation. Javier frowns and goes to write down *food and oxygen* but stops when he sees me shaking my head.

I try to be more specific. "I was thinking more along the lines of what we need to find the missing trophy."

We're all deep in thought for a minute.

"What if ... to catch a missing football trophy, we have to think like one?" Georgie says, folding her arms. Javier looks at her. I look at her. She might be on to something.

"That's actually not a bad idea." I carry on thinking. *Trophy gets stolen... Football final is just days away.*

"Who would want a football trophy more than anyone?" I say out loud.

"A footballer," Georgie says slowly. "And we've got training today at three p.m."

It's definitely worth exploring. We might

find some clues.

"We'll check out our football team today. And tomorrow we'll see if we can track down this Lilly suspect from Ramsdale. You know where we can find her?" I ask.

"She trains on the green off Albert Road. We'll probably find her there on Saturday morning." Georgie can't even talk about Lilly without rolling her eyes.

This **INVESTIGATION** is heating up. I love it!

"W-wait," Javier stammers. "At three p.m. today, you want *us* to play football?"

Javier is very bad at sports. He once fell over in an egg-and-spoon race. The egg survived but Javier broke his arm in two places. He also sprained his ankle playing *FIFA*.

"Relax, Javier. Your heightened fear is making my eyes water." Georgie scrunches up her face.

I try to reassure him. "Yeah, we got this. It's just a bit of exercise."

"But Georgie says I run like an angry

woodland fairy..." Javier says and groans. (It's true – he does. His arms flail around like he's swatting at mosquitoes.)

Strangely, it doesn't help when Georgie tries to comfort him.

"Don't worry, Javier. A few kicks to the shins, elbows and ribs never hurt anybody."

We both look at her. *Come on, bro.*

When Georgie was a baby, her dummy fell out. She caught it on the volley, did three kick-ups and flicked the dummy right back into her mouth. Right now, me and Javier both look like babies (and not ones who are good at football). We're wearing old, too-small PE kits that we found in Lost Property and standing awkwardly on the sidelines of the football field.

"Javier, stop sucking your thumb and playing with your earlobe." Honestly!

Georgie's already out on the pitch, warming up. Seriously, she's a **MAGICIAN** with that ball. She kicks it super high into the air. *WHACK.*

Waits three seconds...

Two...

One.

And then touches down on her left foot with ease.

Mr Ed Herring the coach calls us all over. His power is that he can turn invisible when nobody's watching him.

Margaret Chow's here too. She's the **REFEREE**, and she keeps blowing the whistle when it's not needed – especially given the game hasn't started yet. Her black-and-white outfit is buttoned right to the top. You can tell she's taking this very seriously.

Mr Ed Herring puts me and Javier on Georgie's team to even out the numbers, and training begins.

We're dreadful. I go to kick the ball with my left foot, and it just hits my right foot and rolls away. This is harder than it looks. At least I'm trying though. When the ball goes near Javier, he turns in the opposite direction and runs away. At one point, the ball rolled past and he screamed and ducked behind me like a cartoon elephant hiding from a mouse.

Even with us two playing, you can tell that our school team is overpowering. Literally. All the footballers' powers have made them into some kind of super squad. I list them out in my head – I wonder if any of their special talents are useful for stealing trophies.

Cami Bridgeshire - *kinda scruffy. Her power is amazing vision. It's so good that she can see whether an ant is smiling or not, and she has to wear giant glasses to make her short-sighted.*

Georgie Best - *my best friend. Obviously incredible on the ball. Can also smell fear in her opponents, which she uses to target any weakness in the opposing team.*

Jock Isaacs - new guy. Can turn into a fly. He shrinks down so you can barely see him and then appears out of nowhere to slide-tackle you.

Max Eemam - has one very big, super-strong leg (the other one is normal). Not great at running but could kick the ball into orbit. Has to have his shorts tailor-made.

At half-time, we stop for a big drink of water and some orange slices. I did manage to kick the ball once and I passed it straight to Jock (who wasn't on my team). But, even so, we would be winning if it wasn't for Margaret Chow being the referee.

"She said I was offside even though

I clearly wasn't," Georgie huffs. "Honestly, it's like she doesn't want us to win."

Margaret doesn't want us to win... Georgie is easily our best player, and Margaret did keep blowing the whistle every time Georgie was on the ball. **SUSPICIOUS**. I pull out my list of suspects and add a note next to Margaret's name. She suddenly comes up behind me, carrying a tray, and I shove the list back in my pocket.

"I brought hot chocolate for your refreshment," she says with a big, fake smile. "You must all be pretty tired. Well, most of you." She side-eyes Javier.

"Hey, running away from the ball is just as tiring as running towards it." He frowns while sipping his drink.

Jock looks at the tray of mugs. "When I played for Ramsdale Primary, we never had hot chocolate at half-time. We drank the **TEARS** of our **ENEMIES**," he says.

"Oh yeah? Were your enemies cutting onions on the football pitch?" Georgie replies. Sick burn. "I swear Ramsdale never won a single match against us."

"We would've done if I was captain," Jock blurts out. "I'd be the best captain of any team. Even this one."

"In your dreams," Georgie replies.

"Don't tell me what dreams to dream," he says.

Max, Cami and even Javier jump in and start disagreeing with Jock. Only Margaret stays silent.

Mr Ed Herring comes over and tells us to start getting ready for the second half. Javier groans and puts his face in his hands. To be fair, we don't really have to go back out there. I think I've got everything I need for our investigation.

"Actually, sir, me, Georgie and Javier might have to sit this one out. We're still on the hunt for the stolen trophy."

"Stolen trophy, eh?" he says, stroking his chin.

"That's funny because someone also stole my ham-and-cheese sandwich from the staffroom fridge last week. The plot thickens."

It doesn't.

"So, can we go?" I ask.

"Yes, yes, you three can go," he tells me.

Georgie pulls a face at me like she's frowning. Oh no, maybe I should've asked if she wanted to stay for the rest of the training session. I'll apologise later.

Before I forget, I add Jock's name to the **SUSPECTS LIST**.

* _Jock Isaacs_ – wants to be <u>team captain</u> instead of Georgie. Used to play for <u>Ramsdale</u>. Kind of irritating, like an armpit rash, but less fun to look at.

Suddenly a big drop of water lands on the notebook and smudges some of the ink. Then I feel another droplet on my face. Either Javier is whistling with his mouth full of food again or—

"The clouds are crying! Why are the clouds crying?" Georgie shouts, holding her palm out to confirm. Fat raindrops land on her sleeves, then her shoulders, and suddenly all of us are being drenched. It's like the clouds are hiding a giant showerhead.

Immediately, kids start screaming and running around. It's chaos. People are slipping and sliding in the mud. Max is on his knees, shouting, "*I'M MELTING!*", and "*THE END IS NIGH!*" kid runs past us, screaming.

"It's the sky waters of tales yonder!" Mr
Ed Herring wails.

I'm frozen in shock. It's never rained in
Walsham, not since way before I was born.
More and more rain comes down, soaking us.
But I actually like it – the feeling as it hits my
skin, the smell after it lands. I tilt my head up to
the sky. The only thing I'm worried about is my
hair getting wet.

"Sara, let's go – I don't like it." Javier shivers.
I can't tell if he's cold or terrified. Maybe both.
Behind him, everyone else sloshes around.

"Come *on!*" Georgie shouts to us. She's soaked
through. I don't think she likes the rain either.

While everyone's sprinting back to the
changing rooms for shelter, Georgie grabs me by
the arm and whispers something in my ear.

"Sara, I need to tell you something."

"It's raining – I know."

"No, it's not that." Her voice is shaky. "I could smell fear – really, really strongly – when you were talking about the missing trophy."

Wait, what?

"Could you tell where it was coming from?" I ask.

She nods. The rain has really started pouring down now.

"It was someone on the **TEAM**. One of them knows something."

SATURDAY

(SOUNDS LIKE SAT ALL DAY.)

TODAY WILL NOT BE A DAY
OF SITTING – WE'RE HANGING
POSTERS AND INTERROGATING
CRIMINAL SUSPECTS

Mr Ed Herring? ~~Miss Teree~~ Margaret???
Jock? Kay? Jock! Lilly?!
Lilly?? Kay? Margaret? Jock?
Kay? Margaret?
CHAPTER 6
Kay?
Lilly!
Jock? Margaret! Lilly?
Margaret? Kay! ~~Javier?~~ ← JK!!!

It's finally the weekend, and I keep hoping that
this week's events were all a **BAD DREAM**. The
trophy, the IT room, the rain, all of it. But when
I open my eyes, I see my list of suspects on the
bedside table: Lilly Padd, Margaret Chow, Kay
Lectron and Jock Isaacs.

Deep breath, Sara, you got this. Mum always
says that the early bird gets the worm, and
Dad says the early worm should've stayed
in bed so it didn't get eaten by the early bird.
I think I'm the bird?

76

I head downstairs but I don't have time to talk to Mum and Dad. Gary delivered two gold envelopes this morning. Walsham wasn't built for the rain, and my parents have got all sorts of floods and road-traffic incidents to deal with. They both had to rush off before I could bring up the investigation.

I message the others and we agree to meet up at Georgie's house to plan our day.

Javier's already arrived by the time I get there. Georgie's house is pretty cool: as soon as you step inside, there's an entire wall with medals and mini trophies that Georgie and her parents have won.

We sit in Georgie's kitchen, with a view of her huge garden that's got goalposts at either end. Georgie's parents are watching a match in the living room, so we basically have the house to ourselves. We're drinking orange juice as we decide our next steps in the investigation.

"Javier, do you have the photocopies of the trophy?" I ask him. He said he'd swing by the history classroom to print them off yesterday. He pats his inside pocket to confirm. "And Georgie, can you take us to Albert Road and identify Lilly?"

"Yep. She's the one who's afraid of loud noises and likes ready salted crisps. You can't miss her."

"Great. But, just in case, you can point her out? We'll put up the posters on the way there."

"Sounds like a plan," she replies.

GOODY GUMDROPS, let's go.

Walsham feels different at the weekends, especially today. People in the street keep looking up at the clouds like the sky's about to come ***CRASHING DOWN***. It looks like a big grey ceiling.

Yasmine is huddled in the doorway of her nail

salon, and she takes a moment to acknowledge us before accepting one of our "Missing" posters for her window. She doesn't even glance at it.

I get a closer look though and wow – Javier has done a great job. The lettering is in 3D and he's added my mobile number. He's even sprayed the corners with lavender and signed them in silver pen.

"Javier?"

"Yeah?"

"Sara proud." I put my thumb under my chin. He does the signal back to acknowledge.

We get to work, hanging the posters on lamp posts as we make our way to Albert Road. Me and Javier brought sticky tape. Georgie uses chewed chewing gum. It's a little gross but it gets the job done.

"What's going on here then?" The mayor with the **COLOURFUL FARTS** has seen us and wanders over. He picks up one of the posters. "Oh dear, oh no, how terrible! I'll keep a lookout and let you know if I see anything."

We thank him and carry on walking. We hear, **"THE END IS NIGH!"** as that kid cycles past us.

The local gym instructor who has the power of **SUPER OPTIMISM** comes out of his house, whistling a happy tune. But there's a loud rumble of thunder, so he turns round quickly and goes straight back inside.

Lilly's on the green, ball at her feet, dribbling around cones. As we approach, I tell the others to stay calm. We're just asking questions. This isn't an interrogation.

"Well, well, well," Lilly says, "if it isn't Georgie Surname."

We all look at each other, confused.

Javier nervously asks, "You ... you think her surname is 'Surname'?"

For the record, it isn't. That's just silly.

"Well, my brother's nickname is Nick, so explain that one," she says.

"I mean, I can't," Javier replies, and shuffles backwards.

Georgie's pacing around behind us with her hands in her pockets, like someone in a dance battle waiting their turn. "I guess you win that round, Lilly," she mutters.

There are **no** winners in this interaction. Javier's eyes are darting backwards and forwards like he's at a tennis match.

"Listen, we just have a few questions for you." I take a step forward. "I know you two have history with each other, but we're looking for our missing trophy. If you've got it, please give it back and we can all go home." I'm using my polite voice. Mum says that if you're nice to people, good things tend to happen.

"Trophy?" she says. "What trophy?"

I turn and nod at Javier; he pulls out one of the

posters and hands it to her.

Lilly studies it, one eyebrow raised. "Yeah, this doesn't mean anything to me." She shakes her head, almost apologetically. "And, by the way, we don't have history with each other – we're in different classes? I don't even go to your school."

At that point, Georgie stops pacing behind us and starts screaming at Lilly. "*Just give me back my trophy! Where did you put it?! I will scour the earth! I'll eat a bowl of hair! You want me to eat hair? I'll do it!*"

Whoa. That escalated quickly. Lilly's dropped the poster she was looking at and is now cowering behind Javier. Heh, the irony.

"I don't know anything about a trophy or the guy you're looking for!"

"Guy?"

"Well, yeah – the guy on your 'Missing' poster? I assume you're talking about the man in the picture."

We all look at the poster again; the main image is the pixelated owner bouncing on a see-saw with the trophy perched on the other end. Drats, Lilly does have a point.

Based on her reaction, I don't think she's the one we're looking for. Also, the **STORM** is getting worse so I think we might have to head indoors. Maybe we take the loss on this one.

Plus, Georgie needs a timeout. She's still fuming, breathing so deeply her shoulders are heaving.

We leave Lilly to her football practice and practically drag Georgie away.

This is useless.

"What do we do now, Sara?" Georgie sounds so disappointed now she's calmed down.

"We stick to our plan. Suspects and research," I tell her firmly. "I won't accept defeat. Or de-hands."

I try to hold it in but I giggle at my own joke. They both stare at me with blank faces. There's another loud rumble of **THUNDER** that makes us all jump, and we scurry home.

We've done our posters.

We've interviewed a suspect.

Time for the next phase in our investigation. Let's hope for better results.

Back at Georgie's house, we're sitting in her kitchen with our notebooks out. I've added notes next to Lilly's name on the **SUSPECTS LIST** since our meeting with her. Javier's munching on some toast, sending crumbs flying everywhere, like sand on the way back from the beach.

"I think the next step is to continue our research," I tell them. The rain has got me pretty

shook up, and I peer out into the garden. The sky
looks like concrete.

"If the trophy and the rain are linked, then we
ought to explore that first. We should use the town
library! If the trophy is old, then maybe there'll be
books that were written around the same time.
And we won't be leaving a digital trace."

If Kay is the one behind all this, it's best to keep
our research offline.

Javier gulps. Georgie asks if there's any other
way. "I don't like it when we use ancient tech.
Remember when I built that sundial?"

"Books aren't exactly ancient tech. And that
sundial would've worked if you'd taken it outside.
During the day," I reply.

The town library is a great place to go for
research, and there won't be too many students
on a Saturday. The only problem? Stefano
Lanzani. He's a boy in our year at school whose
dad owns the library. Because of that, he's the
library monitor there (and at school: his dad

donates a lot of money wherever his son goes).
Stefano has a fearsome reputation.

"Some say that he has the power to make
your ⟫ **HEAD EXPLODE** ⟪," Javier says,
biting his lip.

Georgie looks nervous too.

"Yeah, and I heard that
his power can make your
TEETH FALL OUT." She grabs
my shoulders and says, "Sara,
I don't wanna be the kid who
slobbers all over apples. I already
have trouble peeling oranges."

"Well, you can only have one power at a
time," I tell them, "so those things can't both
be true."

We start putting on our jumpers and getting
ready to leave. The rain's begun to die down, and
we're not sure if we'll get another opportunity
to hit the library today. When we're ready, we
gather by the front door.

"We got this?" I zip up my hoodie, quite heroically I think, and turn to Georgie.

"We got this," she confirms, zipping her own hoodie and turning to Javier.

He slowly does up the buttons on his little beige jacket. *Clip. Clip. Clip.* Then he sees the look on our faces. "Erm, yes, we definitely have this. Go, team," he says feebly.

I'll take it.

LET'S BOUNCE.

Walking up the concrete steps to the library, we're all a bit silent. Just inside the entrance are big oak doors. I don't knock immediately. I really wish the others hadn't made such a big deal about Stefano's powers.

"Ugh, Javier, relax. You're starting to smell like a fart's fart," Georgie tells him.

When I do finally knock, one of Stefano's

friends opens the door with a lollipop in his mouth. I think he's in Year Six. He's wearing black shades and has an earpiece like a security guard.

"Roger to Falcon, we have three kids here, over," he says, pressing his finger to his ear. Then he asks me, "What do you want?"

"We've come to see Stefano Lanzani." I try to stop my voice from shaking.

He presses his finger to his ear again. "They're here to see Big Dog." He looks us up and down. "The football girl, the scaredy-cat kid and the one with no powers."

Ouch. I don't bother replying to Roger. This investigation is more important than a zingy comeback. He's just a sidekick who wears silly sunglasses indoors.

He leads us into the library. Rows and rows of books on shelves snake round like a maze. There are a few computers dotted about; the people using them murmur to each other but quickly put their heads down when Roger walks past. Wow, Stefano really scares everyone in here.

"I heard he has the power to **LAUGH LIKE A THOUSAND BABIES**," Javier whispers.

"Not now," I shush him. "And also, what? That sounds adorable."

Georgie is shuffling on the spot when Roger tells us, "Stefano will see you now."

We follow him to the middle of the library where Stefano is sitting on one of those chairs with the wheels on. He's reading a book with a bright green cover but he puts it aside and uses his short legs to swivel round and face us. It's funny that his codename is Big Dog – he looks more like a hamster. A stuffed cushion sits on his lap, and he's stroking it like a cat.

"Welcome to my domain. I am Stefano but you may know me as ... the **LIBRARY MONITOR**." He's very dramatic.

We don't say anything. Javier clears his throat.

"As you're probably aware, nothing in this town gets past me. I know everything. I know the school lunch schedule. I know everyone's powers. I even know the dinner lady's birthday."

How is that relevant? Bah, I don't care. I let him finish. (I like my teeth the way they are.)

"I will give you exactly one minute to state your purpose."

OK, I'm not liking this guy at all. I hesitate before I respond. "Um, yeah, so, we just need to do a bit of research," I tell him.

Stefano sits back in his chair. "And what exactly are you researching?" (Like it's any of his business.)

"The missing trophy at school. We're looking for the culprit." This time I say it with chest.

Stefano looks up at Roger who raises his eyebrows. They both frown. Out of the corner of my eye, I see Georgie slowly bring her hand up to pinch her nose.

"I'm afraid I can't allow that." He shakes his head. Roger gives a little cough. "If the thief finds out you came to me for help—"

"So, you know who it is?" I can't help interrupting him. Is that why these two are acting so **SUSPICIOUSLY**? I make a note to add their names to the list of **SUSPECTS**.

"I didn't say that," he snaps at me. "You know what? I've made up my mind, and no, you can't use the library."

"That doesn't seem fair," I protest.

"If fair was fun and life was fair, we'd all be giggling everywhere."

What does that even mean?

Javier frowns and glances at me. Georgie tilts her head to the side like she's trying to make sense of it. I guess there's no point arguing with this guy. This looks like a **DEAD END**.

"By the way, what's with the cushion on your lap?"

"I spilled minestrone on my trousers."

He removes the cushion to show a big orange stain. "Maybe I could use my powers to get rid of the stain? Of course, I might end up making **YOUR TEETH FALL OUT**." Javier squirms next to me. "Or I might accidentally **BLOW YOUR HEADS OFF**. Maybe I should just see what happens."

Roger raises his eyebrows behind the sunglasses.

Georgie actually **GASPS** out loud, and Javier hides behind me.

"That won't be necessary." I stare him in the eye. He stares back at me. Neither of us move.

"Good choice," Stefano says eventually. "Now, if you'll excuse me, we have important business to attend to. My sources tell me that my mamma just got home from shopping. She's bought those strawberry jelly cups that I like."

"Wibble wobble," Roger says as Stefano waves us away and heads for the doors. Javier flinches and Georgie rolls her eyes.

We're not giving up that easily. We have to

come up with a new strategy. Mum says that panic isn't a substitute for patience. I just need to think for a minute.

Stefano's gone, not that he could *actually* stop us anyway. And we wouldn't need our teeth to do research...

"Guys, he's finally left. We can get on with our research," I tell them. "Let's start in the 'T' section of books to see if there's anything on trophies."

"But we still don't know the dinner lady's birthday," Georgie says.

"Probably June," Javier replies. "She has strong Gemini vibes."

We bump into Max and Jock on our way. Apparently, they're looking for comic books about normal people with no powers, maybe something about a regular person who has a pleasant day at work. We wish them luck in their search.

94

When we get to the right section, we spend the next ten minutes reading all the titles on the shelf, top to bottom, but with no luck.

"I've got a book about treasure, but no trophies," Georgie says, pulling a big, dusty volume from the shelf.

It's a bright green book called *The History of* WALSHAM TREASURE, written by Chloe Isaacs. On the cover there's a whole bunch of shiny objects. One of them could be a trophy. And it is specific to the town.

"I guess that'll have to do for now," I tell them.

We take the book to the librarian to scan. She's tall and has big, curly hair that stands up in all different directions. She's interrupted by

a fly buzzing round her and starts waving her arms about to shoo it away. Then, to style it out, she starts dancing like she's in a trance.

"Erm. OK. Right. Well." I turn to look for an empty table, clutching the book tightly under my arm. It's the only lead we have right now.

We find a space to sit down, somewhere near the back of the library that's getting busier and busier. We're all keeping our heads down in case Stefano or one of his goons reappear.

"What do we do if Stefano comes back?" Javier asks, carefully looking around.

"Duck," I tell him.

"Chicken," Georgie says.

"Goose..." Javier joins in.

I tell them to stop naming farmyard birds and stay alert.

I take out my list of suspects and add Stefano's name and motive.

Suspects List

* Lilly Padd – Ramsdale football captain with motive to <u>sabotage</u> our team, Georgie's nemesis (looking unlikely).

* Margaret Chow – doesn't like us for some reason, especially <u>mean</u> to Georgie.

* Kay Lectron – has read our <u>student files</u>. Possibly knows about Georgie's obsession with the trophy?

* Jock Isaacs – wants to be <u>team captain</u> instead of Georgie. Used to play for Ramsdale. Kind of irritating, like an armpit rash, but less fun to look at.

* Stefano Lanzani – didn't want us doing research. <u>Possibly</u> knows who the thief is.

? ? ? ?

Georgie sees and raises her eyebrows at me.

"You could smell fear on him, couldn't you? When we mentioned that we were looking for the thief," I say.

She nods and pulls a face. "You think he knows who it is?" she says under her breath.

"You heard him. Nothing that happens in this town gets by Stefano Lanzani."

I'm pretty certain that was the only time he was telling us the truth. Either way, Stefano Lanzani is hiding something from us. And we are going to get to the bottom of it.

This is Not a BOOK — Phil Osophy

EASTER EGG — By Nate Lessore

CLOSE CALL — JUSTIN TYME

The History of WALSHAM TREASURE — Chloe Isaacs

CHAPTER 7

Simran Singh's — Drawing Conclusions

The clouds outside are getting darker, and it's raining more often. Drops splatter against the window as we sit in our uncomfortable library chairs. We're going through *The History of* **WALSHAM TREASURE**, looking for clues that link any of our suspects to the stolen trophy. So far, there's nothing. Most of this book is about the mysterious Valkro Strapp, hero of Walsham (and award-winning fingerpaint artist).

We're getting desperate. Georgie's game is just two days away, and she's been biting her nails all morning.

"We'll get it back," I reassure her. We pore over every page but there's nothing in here that we don't already know from history lessons.

"This is the **WORST THING EVER**!" Georgie wails. Javier pats her arm but even he doesn't look hopeful. "I don't wanna be on the first losing team in eighty years." She sobs.

I open my mouth to tell her that she might not lose, because even without good luck we still have the better team.

But something she just said made me think.

Eighty years.

We haven't lost in **EIGHTY YEARS**.

You know what else happened eighty years ago? Valkro came to Walsham.

What if...

No.

But what if...

"Javier, what was the phrase that was inscribed on the trophy? The one you translated from Spanish." I'm gripping the underside of my chair in excitement.

"Something about caves? I gift you powers, but don't move me," he recalls.

"Thanks, you completely amazing human being!"

Javier smiles sheepishly and shrugs. He juts his neck out so I can tickle him under the chin. Dear little Javier.

"Maybe it's not a coincidence that all this weird stuff has been happening since that trophy was moved," I say.

Then I'm racing through

The History of WALSHAM TREASURE.

I turn the pages frantically. Scanning each page. Dust flying out of the book.

Georgie coughs. Her eyes were already watery. We come across one section that describes the treasure's arrival, the object that gives Walsham its powers. I take a very deep breath.

"Soon after Valkro's arrival eighty years ago, the inhabitants of Walsham started noticing changes." I look up at Georgie. "When did you say our school's good luck at football began?"

"Eighty years ago," she whispers.

I jump straight back into the book. "But as soon as the treasure left Walsham a **DARK CLOUD** appeared over the town for the first time since its arrival. Thus began ... the **PLAGUES OF WALSHAM**."

Georgie covers her face with her hand. Javier's gone white as a sheet.

"P-p-plagues?" he stammers.

I start reading them out:

No Sunday roast.
Dark clouds and rainfall.
No tea.
No more orderly queues.
Storms rage throughout.

I gulp before reading out the last part.

"On the fifth day of the treasure's absence, the most **POWERFUL RAINSTORM** hit the town, and all its inhabitants started **LOSING THEIR POWERS**." Now my stomach's just gone cold. I soldier on. "Experts predicted that by 5 p.m. on day five, everyone in Walsham would lose their gifts. And then the town would become like any other boring town. Such as Doncaster."

Everything that makes Walsham **SPECIAL** would be no more. The first two plagues match the strange school lunch and all the weird weather. "When the treasure goes missing, so do the gifts within."

When I turn the page, I almost fall off my chair. It's a picture of Valkro Strapp, the first time any of us has seen him properly. Bright, smiling eyes and a thick moustache.

"Is that ... the guy on our poster?" Javier asks.

The quality in this picture is much better than our dark and grainy image, but I'm pretty sure it's him. My heart is drumming away in my chest.

"The treasure is the trophy. The trophy is the treasure." I flop back in my chair. "The treasure's gone missing. The whole town is gonna lose their powers." What does that mean for the rest of Walsham?

"And there are only five days until that happens? What is that in hours and minutes?" Georgie shrieks, trying to do the maths in her head.

"It's 120 hours or 7,200 minutes," Javier responds.

"Wow, that was incredible," she says in shock. "OMG, is that your power? Instant maths?"

"No, I just used a calculator," he says, holding up his phone.

I tell them that it doesn't matter how many days it is *in total*, it's how many days we have *left*.

Thursday – trophy went missing, first cloud appeared, no Sunday roast.

Friday – rain started.

Saturday – today.

That only leaves us with **Sunday** and until 5 p.m. on **Monday** to find the trophy!

Suddenly there's lots murmuring around the library. A few people walk over to a screen on the wall to watch a breaking news story.

The kid who shouts "***THE END IS NIGH!***" is quickly shushed by everyone. A girl points at the TV and unmutes it, using her powers.

The reporter looks worried and is shuffling papers. "BREAKING NEWS – Walsham is experiencing an electrical appliance pandemic. Kettles all over the town are malfunctioning, even the new ones. Nobody has been able to make a cup of tea, and we've not got anything to dunk our biscuits into." The news presenter holds up a broken kettle. "This is not a drill. I repeat, this is not a drill." And then she quietly says, "It's a kettle."

BREAKING NEWS BREAKING NEWS BREAKING NEWS

Georgie and Javier turn to look at me. "No tea," we say together.

This is big. Our case involves a whole lot more than a simple school theft. This **CHANGES EVERYTHING** to do with our investigation. It's not about football, it's about Valkro's treasure. We have to update our Suspects List, keeping in mind the new **MOTIVES**, and which one of them would've known about the **PLAGUES**.

Updated Suspects List

* Margaret Chow – was <u>very attentive</u> in history class. Seemed to know a lot about Valkro Strapp.

* Kay Lectron – has <u>all</u> the knowledge of the internet at their disposal.

* Jock Isaacs – ex-player for Ramsdale (and wished he had been their captain). No powers for everyone in Walsham could mean their <u>first win</u>?

* Stefano Lanzani – claims to know <u>everything</u> about everything.

I didn't include Lilly's name in our new list. Our interrogation showed that she had no idea about the trophy, let alone that it was the treasure.

I can't believe all of this – **PLAGUES**, **THUNDERSTORMS** and **NO MORE POWERS**. What's gonna happen to my parents, and everyone in the IPA, on day five? You can't be a superhero if you don't have superpowers. I'll never know what it's like to **SAVE THE DAY**. I'll never make my mum and dad proud the same way they make me proud every day. Oh, this is a disaster!

???

When I get home, the first thing I do is flick the kettle switch on and off. Nothing happens. I slump at the kitchen table.

Mum and Dad both arrive at the same time. Dad comes **CRASHING** through the front door, and Mum **GLIDES GRACEFULLY** over the house and lands in the back garden.

"You OK, munchkin?" Dad asks when he sees me hunched over the table.

I shake my head. How could they understand? They're both out there rescuing people, while I'm just a normie with no powers and no way of saving the town. They exchange a look and sit down either side of me.

"Is it to do with your powers again? You wanna talk about it?" Mum's voice is delicate. I shrug my shoulders. "Is it something to do with that case you've been working on? The one for Georgie?" *Sigh*.

"Well, the thing is..." I start telling them about the trophy, how it's actually **VALKRO STRAPP'S TREASURE**, and my list of suspects. I explain how all these plagues are gonna get worse, and that everyone's gonna lose their powers.

I'm secretly hoping that my parents both jump up out of their chairs and say something like, "Well, what are we waiting for? Let's all go find that treasure – there's no time to waste!" and then they save the day while I just sit and eat crisps in front of the telly.

"Sara, are you sure about this?" Dad shoots a worried look at Mum who sits back in her chair with her hands pressed together.

I nod.

Mum doesn't respond straight away, and when she does she talks really slowly. "Well, that explains the grey skies. We need to report this back to the IPA. If it is true, the entire town is in jeopardy." She turns to me. "You've done some great detective work here."

"Yes, don't give up. You got this, sweetie," Dad adds.

Am I missing something? Why are they not as anxious as I am?

"Guys, is that it?" I look up at them. "The whole town is going to lose their **SPECIAL GIFTS**. Even you. I don't have *any* powers. I'm useless. What's gonna happen to the IPA on day five, to all the people that need your help?" They're really not taking this seriously enough.

"Honey, we're as scared as you are but it's important to stay calm. Nobody solves problems by stressing," Mum says.

Dad is nodding along. Why are they so logical all the time?

"You already have a list of suspects," he says. "You've been following clues, and your friends are helping out."

My days, this is horrible. My heart is beating really fast. Why won't they understand? I look down at my lap. "I might fail."

"And you might not," Dad says brightly.

"It's OK to fail," Mum chimes in.

"But, Mum, I don't want you guys to lose your powers." My lip is trembling. "I'm scared."

"And it's OK to be scared. Me and your father get scared all the time," she says firmly.

"You do?" They've never told me that before.

"Of course we do. **BRAVERY** isn't the absence of fear. Bravery is when you keep doing what's right, even if it terrifies you. Listen, without *any* powers, you've done so much already, and you're still here," Mum says.

Dad stands up. "Sara, did I ever tell you about the time I pulled a two-ton coach out of a river?"

"Yeah, you only used one hand because you were texting Mum about dinner." I've heard this story before. He saved twenty people that day.

"That's true but I didn't tell you about Robert, the driver. He saved two people before I even got there, swam back down to save more." I didn't know that part. Dad's face is serious now, his mind back with that coach. "My point is," he continues, "that Robert didn't have any powers. He was from London. Do you think he's less of a hero because he only saved two people and I saved twenty?"

"No, Dad." I feel bad about my moaning.

"You know who else didn't have powers?" he asks.

I smile a bit. He always does this to cheer me up. "Emmeline Pankhurst, Nelson Mandela and Martin Luther King," I tell him.

"Who else?" he says, grinning.

"Queen Victoria, Marcus Rashford and ... all the Barbies!" We both fall about laughing while Mum grins at us.

When the laughter dies down, Dad's got his serious face on again. "So, what's going to be your next move?"

I'm picturing everything in my head: Kay's IT room, the story of Valkro's treasure, the football game... What do they all have in common?

I pull out the **SUSPECTS LIST** and see Margaret Chow's name. She was in Kay's IT room that day. And in history class she did know an awful lot about the treasures and powers. She clearly dislikes Georgie, and looks at her the same way I look at anchovies on a pizza. She seems to have the strongest motive.

"Margaret has a rubbish power, sensing dogs' emotions," I say out loud. "Could it be so rubbish that she wouldn't care if the whole town lost out?" I'm stroking my chin. "Sounds ruff."

Haha, *ruff*. Pause for laughter.

"Heh, paws for laughter?" I try again. The kitchen is silent. Dad clears his throat.

But then I get another burst of excitement when I think about how much me and Margaret are always beefing. Could she be *my* **NEMESIS**? If she is, then proving she stole the trophy might **KICKSTART** my superpower. Maybe I can still join the IPA.

Mum and Dad put their arms round me. "Go get 'em, munchkin."

The fate of tea depends on me!

114

CHAPTER 8

"What are we doing today again?" It's Sunday and Georgie's sitting in my room, caked in mud from her football training this morning. She's **BOUNCING** up and down on the bed while I explain the plan *again*. (Fourth time lucky.)

"We're gonna tail Margaret Chow, on the down-low."

"Down low? You want us to crouch?"

"No..." I try to explain. "We'll be following Margaret from afar, to see if she leads us to the trophy's hiding place. Now where's Javier with those disguises?"

He finally gets here, climbing in through my bedroom window instead of using the door like a normal person. That kid is so weird. But I race over to see what he's got in his rucksack. Me and Georgie are clapping our hands together in excitement as he opens it.

"This is for you," he says, grinning happily, and pulls out a newspaper with two small circles cut out to use as eyeholes.

Georgie holds it up to her face. "Do you think Margaret will recognise me?" she says.

Hmm. Let's not panic just yet. "Javier, do you have anything else in there?"

He nods and takes out a tree branch.

I look at it, then I look at him. "Is that supposed to be a disguise? You had *one* job..."

"You can hide behind it." He starts waving the branch around. "I was thinking we could follow Margaret, and if she turns round you can crouch and pretend you're a bush."

117

"Javier, I thought you were bringing disguises. So far, you've got a newspaper with holes in it and a stick." We're not off to a strong start with this **MISSION**. "Please tell me you've got something else in there."

He bites his lip and hesitates before diving back into his rucksack. He pulls out a big handful of deflated purple balloons.

My mouth drops open when he hands them to me. I scan his face. "Javier," I say quietly. "What in the name of Costco John-Bosco am I supposed to do with those?"

Nothing to see here!

"I was thinking we could blow them all up and attach them to me, then I'd be disguised as a bunch of grapes."

"Oh well, that's just great. I'm sure Margaret

won't see through our grapes and our sticks," I say,
holding the tree branch up to my face.

"Who said that?" Georgie asks, looking around.

We're camped across the road from the bakery,
where a **CROWD** is forming instead of a **QUEUE**.
Usually, people wait in line but this is a mess.
Margaret Chow's been in there for five minutes,
and it looks like nobody's getting served
in the chaos. "**THE END IS NIGH!**"
kid comes out screaming because he
couldn't buy his doughnuts. I dough-not
want to be him right now.

OK. Enough hilarious jokes.

Javier's got his branch. Georgie has the
newspaper. I'm wearing a hoodie and a cap
pulled low over my face. Javier brought the
balloon disguise in his pocket, just in case.

"What do you think she's doing in there?"

he whispers, holding up a pair of binoculars.

"You think she's hidden **VALKRO'S TREASURE** in a sausage roll?" Georgie whispers back.

I don't get why they're whispering. Margaret's across the road, indoors, and the traffic out here is super loud. The rain makes it even more unlikely she'd hear us.

None of us are used to being this damp. It's as if we've been standing in the shower with our clothes on. This rain feels light and misty though, like I just sneezed upwards and stayed on the spot.

"Margaret hasn't hidden the school trophy in a sausage roll," I assure them. "That's physically impossible. Plus, I don't think that's how she rolls." I laugh at my own joke. The others don't. Maybe they didn't hear me – it is loud out here.

"OK, there she is," I say, changing the subject.

When she comes out, Margaret takes a left into the shoe shop. She comes out holding a bag with something in it. What could she be doing?

We tiptoe along the other side of the street, a few paces behind her, watching the back of her head bob up and down as she walks. All of a sudden...

She stops dead in her tracks. It looks like she's going to cross the road. We're too close – she's gonna spot us. We all freeze. She stands completely still, then takes two deep breaths. And lets out a **_GIANT SNEEZE_**.

For a second, I think the coast is clear but Margaret wipes her snotty hands on her jeans, and Georgie lets out a giant "_Yeeeeuuuk_, that was gross!" making Margaret spin round.

Javier quickly closes his eyes and holds up his branch. I jump behind a lamp post but ninety-nine per cent of me is still visible. Georgie crouches on the ground and her newspaper blows away in the wind like a big, angry butterfly.

121

Thankfully, just as Margaret Chow turns to face us, a huge lorry stops in the road, blocking us from sight.

As it drives off again, we see that Margaret has carried on down the street, bouncing as she walks.

"Phew. That was a close one," Georgie says. "By the way, Javier, you couldn't lend me a tree branch, could you? My disguise blew away when we almost got caught just then."

He opens his bag but all he's got in there are the purple balloons. "I don't have any more branches with me – they don't grow on trees, you know."

I step in to stop them bickering. If this continues, we'll never complete the mission.

"Guys, she's getting away. And branches *do* grow on trees, pretty much exclusively," I tell them.

Margaret's just turned the corner and is now out of sight. We hurry across the road silently to catch up with her. Man, this would be so much easier if we had **INVISIBILITY POWERS**. Fun fact: my uncle Tim has invisibility, and he uses it every time my aunt Tara asks him to unload the dishwasher.

Margaret Chow turns into the park. She hasn't spotted us yet. Still, we have to be extra careful because the park in Walsham can get a little hectic. People jogging can go as fast as a car, or a stray frisbee could knock your head off. There are **LITTLE EXPLOSIONS OF COLOUR**, people getting stuck in trees if they're gliding too high. Loud **BANGS** and **WHOOSHES** fill the air where picnics take place and tiny kids run around.

123

We spot Margaret marching off the trail towards a patch of trees. I quickly signal to Georgie and Javier to stop. Margaret looks around once, then twice, before disappearing into the bushes.

"OMG, guys, this is it!" My mind is racing and so is my chest. "Margaret Chow, **SUSPECT NUMBER ONE**, is going into her secret park hiding place."

"Rather **SUSPICIOUSLY**," Georgie adds.

We sneak towards the bushes, very careful not to make a noise. When we approach, the trees shade us from the sunlight. The loud noises from the park feel much quieter now, further away. We hear grunting and groaning and low thuds coming from a little opening where we see...

"Margaret Chow –" I jump out – "we knew you were up to something!"

She looks up, terrified, and falls back on to her bottom. "We?"

"Margaret Chow!" Georgie shouts as she
bursts through and joins us.

OK, well, it would've been nice if we'd timed
that properly. In my head, all three of us come
out at the same time, but no, yeah, this is cool.

Javier follows behind Georgie with his hands in
his pockets. Margaret looks up at the three of us,
eyes wide. She's been **BUSTED**.

"So, where is it?" I ask.

"I don't understand – where's what?" she says,
trembling.

"The trophy. Where's the trophy?" I say, looking around. It must be here somewhere. She stares up at me blankly. "Listen, Margaret, if we don't get it back by tomorrow, the whole town will lose its powers. All these **PLAGUES** – the kettles, the rain, everything – they're all connected to that stupid cup. It's **VALKRO STRAPP'S HIDDEN TREASURE**."

"Please, I swear, I don't know what you're talking about!"

I look over at Georgie who nods and takes one step forward. She sniffs the air. "That's fear all right," she confirms.

Margaret Chow looks at me, then at Georgie, then Javier. She opens her mouth, then closes it. "OK," she finally says. "I didn't come here for some silly trophy."

Georgie clenches her fist. Nobody insults a football trophy, especially when its disappearance is **DOOMING** the town.

Margaret looks down at her lap. "I came

here to practise my kick-ups. I'm tired of being a referee. I just want to be part of the football team. I was hoping to join the squad for the final."

"Oh." I don't know what else to say. I guess it makes sense why she doesn't like Georgie, the team captain who never gave her a chance. It's a good **MOTIVE** but I'm not sure it has anything to do with the trophy. "Hold up. If you were practising kick-ups, where's the football?"

"It rolled off into those bushes before you jumped out at me. I'm not very good." She points to where the ball went.

I feel my heart sink. Not because I feel sorry for her but because I actually believe her. If she's not lying, it means she can't really be my **NEMESIS** after all, and I'm no closer to finding **MY SUPERPOWER** or the **TROPHY**.

Javier wanders over to the spot where she pointed and comes back a few seconds later with the ball under his arm. Sugarplums, she was telling the truth.

"Sorry," I mumble with my hands in my pockets.

"Yeah, sorry, Margaret Chow," Javier adds. "The sticks and grapes were my idea."

She does an *oh* face like she has no idea what he's talking about. (Because she doesn't.)

Me and Javier turn to leave but Georgie hesitates. She goes over and holds out her hand to help Margaret up. "If you want, I can help you practise. Our team is already stacked but you can still come on as a substitute if someone gets injured," she tells her.

"I'd like that. Wow, thank you. And hey, did you say that dusty trophy is Valkro Strapp's hidden treasure? *The* Valkro Strapp?" Margaret claps like an excited seal of approval. Then her smile drops when she remembers the plagues I mentioned. "Look, I'd really like to help you find it. I don't want anyone to lose their gifts. Walsham is my home too."

Margaret looks at me, hopeful. I hesitate and turn to Georgie.

"Maybe she could actually be useful," Georgie says under her breath.

"Useful how? Most of the time she's a busy know-it-all," I reply. "What do you think we should do, Javier?"

"I guess time is running out," he says.

"Yeah, and we need all the help we can get. Four heads are better than three," Georgie adds.

"Fine. But if she slows us down it's on you." I turn to Margaret Chow. "We're going back to mine to figure out our next move. You can join us."

"Yes. I know. You guys just had that whole conversation right in front of me. You didn't even step away," she says.

Right. Well.

We start heading back to my house to formulate a new plan. As we step out of the bushes, Margaret Chow is still going on. "You barely lowered your voices. And even if you had, my doctor says I have almost perfect hearing."

I'm regretting this already.

"Sometimes I swear I can hear ants pooping, that's how sharp my hearing is."

If that's true, I'm almost kind of jealous.

Wait, no, I'm not. Why would I want to hear ants pooping?

I take out my list and concentrate on that. My heart sinks as I cross Margaret Chow's name off.

As it stands, our suspects are:

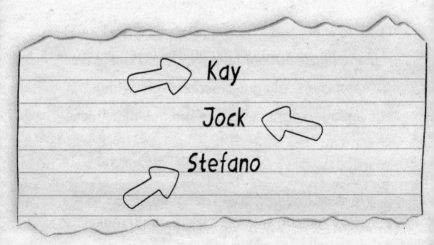

I know I should be happy that we've eliminated another suspect but I can't help feeling a little disappointed that we haven't solved the case.

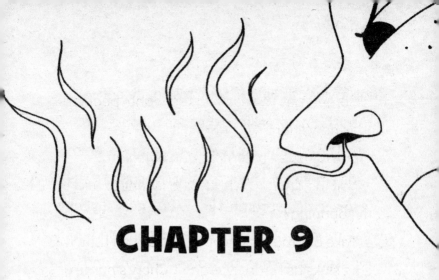

CHAPTER 9

"OK, Javier, let's try this again. Tell Georgie two truths and one lie."

We're all in my bedroom, including Margaret Chow (I dare her to laugh at my posters). I've decided that if we're gonna **SAVE WALSHAM**, we really need to hone our powers. Or *their* powers.

If Georgie can smell the lie, it would make our interrogations much quicker. We need to breeze through our Suspects List if we're gonna catch the culprit in time to save the town and win that football game on Monday. The only problem is that Javier's finding his one task quite difficult.

"Truth: I don't believe that the moon is real. Truth: I hate trifle. Lie: I wear roller skates on my hands whenever I hear a violin," he says.

I take a deep breath. I know he's nervous but we're running out of time. "Javier, you're not supposed to tell us which are the truths and which is the lie. You're missing the point." I rub my eyes. "And I have so many questions about what you just said."

"Yeah, how could you not like trifle?" Georgie asks.

We need a different approach. I tell Margaret to give it a go. She is being helpful but I still can't help rolling my eyes when she straightens up and clears her throat.

"I can do a handstand for three minutes. I have perfect attendance at school. My dad got me a pony for my birthday."

She's so annoying. I really hope she's lying about the pony.

132

I look over at Georgie who is sniffing intensely.
She shrugs, shakes her head and stamps her
feet. "Sara, I can't do this." Georgie groans.
"I'm never gonna get this in time. The only
thing I'm good for is scoring hat-tricks and
gliding past defenders."

I see her lip **TREMBLE**, and quickly put my
hand on her shoulder. "Don't worry. You don't
have to do it if you don't want to. I'm sorry,
guys. I'm getting stressed, and it's not fair on

you." We need a Plan B – I don't want to see anyone upset.

Georgie takes a deep breath in and out. "No, let me try one more time," she says.

Javier gives her an encouraging nod. I tell her to try closing her eyes – maybe shutting off her other senses might help. Margaret Chow goes again, the same two truths and a lie.

With her eyes still closed, Georgie calmly smells the air. "The lie is the handstand," she tells us before opening them again.

"OMG, yes, you got it! I can do a handstand for much longer than three minutes." Margaret squeals with delight. Georgie blushes and grins as we give her a pat on the back. I'm so proud.

"What does it smell like?" I ask her.

"It smells kinda like normal fear but when she lied it was a lot sharper. Like how salt and vinegar crisps smell stronger than ready salted." That is so cool.

I smile at Margaret. "Thank goodness you were

here. Javier had no idea how to play the game."

"Yes, I did," he protests.

Georgie closes her eyes and sniffs him. "**LIE**,"
she says loudly. This is great.

"Does anyone else wanna try their powers out? It might come in handy for tomorrow," I ask Javier and Margaret Chow.

Margaret closes her eyes and puts her fingers to the side of her head. OMG, I've never seen her use her power before. We wait silently, patiently, and then she says, "Your neighbour's dog likes fetching stuff." She brings her hands down and looks round with a smile.

Holy hound dogs, that was disappointing. But we need to encourage each other.

"Wow, Margaret, that was objectively not a waste of time." I guess that's sort of true. "Javier? You wanna give it a go?"

Javier's eyes look around the room and up at the ceiling. "I can't practise in here. I don't have enough space," he says.

"Javier, what *is* your power?" Georgie asks.

He shuffles nervously. He looks like he's going to say something but then he stops and stares at us as if we're about to interrupt him.

"Well?" Georgie asks him expectantly.

But just as Javier opens his mouth to tell us, my mum bursts into the room.

"Sara, it's teatime. Your jollof rice is getting cold. Are your friends eating with us? I can fly over to the supermarket and get apple pies for dessert." She's still in her **SUPERHERO COSTUME**. The neck is frayed and one of the sleeves is torn.

Georgie's belly **RUMBLES** and Margaret Chow is licking her lips as we all bundle out of my room. Margaret whispers, "Your mum is so cool," and I can't help but smile.

MONDAY

SHORT FOR **MUNDANE**, LONG FOR **NO REASON**.

CHAPTER 10

I could barely sleep last night. First of all, today's Monday – **DAY FIVE OF THE CURSE** – and there's the **BIG FOOTBALL FINAL**. What really hurts too is that the people of this town are about to lose their special powers before I've even had a chance to discover mine.

Also a **DEAFENING THUNDERSTORM** started around midnight. The howling wind and flashes of lightning had me hiding under the blanket. I'm glad Georgie wasn't there to smell me.

The storm was so bad that car alarms were

going off, and bins were blown over in the street like they were bowling skittles. When I got out of bed to check outside, I noticed lots of other people standing at their windows looking worried. Mum always says that suffering is a tool for growth and patience, inevitable as the sunrise.

"Growth and patience," I repeat to myself. It helps.

At breakfast, Dad is already suited up for a long day's work. Another large pile of golden envelopes was delivered this morning. He'll be moving the trees that have fallen on to the train tracks, which, with his super strength, might as well be toothpicks. After that, he has to go round picking up any caravans that have toppled over, then a trip to the barber's to shape his beard. For the rest of the day, he'll be carrying any lorries or tractors out of the flooded areas.

Mum gives him a kiss on the cheek and wishes him luck. She'll be gliding around, whooshing all the broken glass and debris into heaps, like

HA! Take **that** storm!

a gardener blowing leaves into a pile. Then she'll spend the rest of her day up in the sky, redirecting the **STORMY WINDS** away from Walsham.

We really need to find this treasure now. Superpowers or not, today's the day we **UNMASK** the **TROPHY THIEF**.

???

Our first stop when we're back at school after the weekend is the IT room. We would've confronted Kay sooner, but none of us know where they spend the weekends. Plus, they kind of have a ... short fuse. (Little electrical joke.)

I'm starting to think amazing jokes probably aren't my superpower, but that won't stop me making them because I'm hilarious.

When Kay opens the door, they look kinda

surprised to see us. They don't let us in.

"Well, well, well, I haven't seen you guys since you accused me of **SABOTAGE** and ran out of here. I let you come in to use these facilities and you left without even saying thank you."

"That's because you turned our machine off." Javier steps forward. Kay looks him up and down, tiny sparks appearing in their eyes as they flash with anger. Javier gulps.

"I did no such thing. What reason would I have to sabotage you?" Now Kay's talking to me.

I tell them about how we were halfway through our research and, just when things were getting juicy, the computers were turned off.

Kay frowns for a minute while they think. "That's right, ALL the machines were turned off, not just yours. I didn't sabotage you."

We're not buying it.

"Then why did you kick everyone out of the IT room?" I ask them.

I clench my fists. There's something they're not

telling us – it can't have been a coincidence.

We stare at each other for ages but then Kay sighs and looks away. "OK, fine. I'll be honest with you," they say.

This is it.

What time is it? **CONFESSION** time.

"I was standing there and a fly went up my nose," Kay says quietly. "It made me sneeze."

Me, Georgie and Javier just stare at them. "When I sneeze, all the electronics do a system reboot." They shake their head. "I can't help it. It's my gift and my curse."

Um. I look at Javier and Georgie, who just shrug at me.

"Wait, so that all happened because you sneezed?"

I unclench my fists. It's starting to look like the whole thing was an accident.

"Yeah, I didn't want to say anything before.

I'm in Year Five – I should have more control of my powers." They hold up their hand to show the sparks on their fingertips. "I was so embarrassed, I just wanted everyone to leave." They suddenly frown and take a big step back from Georgie, who's sniffing them. "Erm, why are you smelling me? Even for you, that's not normal."

"They're telling the truth," Georgie confirms, ignoring Kay.

"What are you, a **HUMAN LIE DETECTOR**? I just told you what happened. Everything else is nunya," they say.

"Nunya?" Georgie asks.

"Yes, as in nunya business." Kay grins at their own joke. (I hate it when people do that.) "Now, if you'll excuse me, we're tracking that lightning over Walsham. The **ELECTRICAL CURRENT** in the air is like nothing I've ever seen before."

In our form room, I cross Kay's name off our Suspects List.

Great. That just leaves Jock and Stefano.

We're all on low energy, except Georgie whose legs are shaking. I've never seen her this nervous. Usually when it comes to football, she's proper confident that she'll bang the goals in like nothing. Today she's sweating buckets, and she keeps checking her PE kit to make sure her football boots are in there. Our school team hasn't lost a single match since that trophy appeared in our school, and the pressure's getting to her.

Poor Georgie :-(

We take it in turns trying to reassure her, telling her that trophy or no trophy she's an absolute **BEAST** on the football pitch. And anyway, we have a plan.

"Georgie, you'll be bossing it at the football final. Keep an eye on Jock, and if you see or smell anything suspicious, text me and we'll rush over," I tell her. Georgie nods but I can still see her leg trembling under the table. "Javier, you'll come with me to the library. We need to look something up, and then I think we should have another chat with Stefano. He definitely knows something, so we have to get him to tell us. We got this." We high-five each other.

"What should I do?" Margaret Chow asks. She's just come into the form room, abandoning her friends to join us. I'm not used to her being here.

"Are you sure you don't wanna go with Georgie? You can still be a substitute."

"No," she says. "You guys need me more than the football team. Georgie's got this." She looks over at Georgie and smiles. "I believe in you." I guess it is sweet that she's being encouraging.

"Fine. Well, in that case, you can come with Javier and I," I tell her.

"Javier and me," she corrects me. I shoot her a look. I'm regretting this already. "Sorry. Old habits."

We say goodbye to Georgie and wish her luck. As we leave, I hear Javier say to Margaret Chow, "I'm very glad that you're coming with I and Sara."

Hurrying down the corridor on the way to the library, I'm explaining our next moves. "I've been thinking about the book we borrowed, *The History of* WALSHAM TREASURE. It gave us a bunch of clues about the trophy.

But the book itself could be the biggest clue of all – someone else must have known that the trophy is the treasure."

Margaret Chow clocks on quicker than Javier. "Maybe there's a copy in the school library – someone could have borrowed it."

"Exactly. It would tell us who else could've known the truth."

The library is **GLOOMIER** than I've ever seen it before. It's never been this dark outside during the day. The bookshelves are long and shadowy. The lights in here look dim and dusty, almost like they've never been used.

Javier and Margaret Chow follow me past rows and rows of books. Thunder rumbles in the distance but at least there's no hurricane like last night. Mum must be up in the clouds doing her job.

We head over to the librarian's desk at the end of a row. As we approach, there's a **LOUD CRACK OF LIGHTNING** outside, and she appears directly behind her desk, eyes bulging, pointing a long finger at us. It would be a creepy entrance except she's halfway through a ham sandwich and chokes on it a little bit. Javier has to go and firmly pat her on the back, and she quietly thanks him.

I take a few steps forward and ask the librarian my questions. "We're looking for a book," I tell her. "*The History of* WALSHAM TREASURE."

"Ah yes, I believe it was returned earlier today." She strokes the hairs on her chinny chin chin.

"Can you tell us who the last person was who borrowed it?" My voice is shaking.

She has a look on her computer. "I'm afraid not. That information isn't in the system," she says apologetically.

Gah. OK. What do we do? Mum says that people who look for problems will always find them, but people who look for solutions will always find those too.

"Let's take a look at the copy that was returned," I say to the others. "Maybe they got sloppy, left us a clue or something."

I'm trying to sound **CONFIDENT** but I'm not sure if it's working. This is how I felt when I had to spell *onomatopeeyah* in my spelling bee.

We scan the shelves, desperate for a hint of green. Margaret looks like she's found it, quickly pulling a book out and holding it up.

"Is this it?" she asks. Then she pulls a disgusted face and looks down at her hand. "*Uuuugh, what is that?*" She starts wiping her palm on her crisp, clean skirt. "It looks like orange goo."

I carefully take the book from her. I sniff the orange substance that's smeared on the back and corners of some of the pages. "That's not goo," I tell her. "That's **MINESTRONE SOUP**. They don't serve it in the school canteen, and there's only one person I've ever seen eating it here at school."

He's a **LIBRARY MONITOR**, so he could have messed with the school system and deleted his name from the record. I know that he got all flustered and shut us down when we told him we were looking for the **TROPHY THIEF**. And I know how to find him.

It's time to pay Stefano Lanzani a visit.

149

CHAPTER II

It has to be Stefano, that thieving, snivelling little toad-in-the-hole. I don't care if he has the power to make my teeth fall out, I'm gonna find him and get the treasure back. I'll pelt him with loose teeth until he tells me what I need to know.

I check my watch. It's 3 p.m. so the football match should be starting soon. "Guys, we only have two hours left!" I tell the others.

"Two hours till no more powers?" Javier asks.

"Yes, no more powers including ours. Meanwhile the whole town cowers," I tell him.

Margaret Chow confidently steps forward with her finger in the air. "Well then, let's scour the hour of the... No, wait, sorry, guys – I dropped it." She shakes her head.

Gah, we don't have time for this!

We track Stefano down in the languages department. He's easy to find – his goons are always loitering in the corridors. The sky outside is darker than ever, and I picture my poor mum up in the clouds redirecting all that wind. We need to find the trophy NOW before things get even worse. I barge straight past Roger and into the classroom.

Stefano is standing by the window, his hands behind his back as he looks out at all the chaos he started.

"Ah, Sara, you've finally figured it out," he says without turning round.

A **_BOLT OF LIGHTNING_** flashes across the sky, and Stefano gives a little scream and ducks down with his hands over his head. He quickly straightens up with his hands behind his back, pretending it never happened.

When he turns and spots Margaret, he raises an eyebrow. "I see you've recruited Miss Chow to your little investigation. Well, it's too late. You're on day five and soon enough everyone will **_LOSE THEIR POWERS_**. Walsham will be like any other place in England. It will finally become a *normal* town and—"

"Where's the trophy?" I interrupt him. I'm not in the mood for these silly games.

Roger takes a step forward but Stefano waves at him to stand down. "It doesn't matter where the trophy is," he says. "You're so concerned with 'where', you never stopped to ask yourself 'why'."

Oh goodness. He's doing that thing where the villain explains their whole life story and all the stupid reasons why they committed the crime.

"For years, I've been at this school, watching day after day as students with these **AMAZING GIFTS** go about their lives. My father couldn't wait to see what mine was, what I'd be able to do. But alas, the hand I was dealt was not what we expected." He scowls, his voice getting louder and louder with every word.

"Listen, whatever your gift is, the whole town doesn't have to suffer because of it," I tell him. I'm gonna ignore the fact that he just said "alas" because, well, who talks like that?

"Gift? GIFT?" he repeats. "You want to know what my 'gift' is? You want to know why I did what I did? Behold the true power of Stefano Lanzani!"

He reaches his hand up.

Javier dives for cover. Margaret Chow flinches. I watch in horror as Stefano pinches the end of his nose and puffs out his cheeks.

For a split second, nothing happens. But then **COLOURFUL BUBBLES** come streaming out of his ears. Just happy little bubbles, some of them landing with a gentle pop.

Javier opens one eye. And then the other. He straightens up and looks at me, confused. Stefano releases his nose as the last few bubbles drift away into nothingness.

"What about the teeth falling out? Or m-making people's heads explode?" Javier stammers.

"*I* started those rumours. My power is so useless, my dad had to pay *him* to be my bodyguard." He nods at Roger. "Nobody would take me seriously if they knew the truth."

Right, because someone who uses words like "alas" and spills minestrone on his lap should defo be taken seriously.

Stefano turns back to look out of the window. "I waited for my opportunity. And when my father put me in charge of the library I was approached by my accomplice, a true **MASTERMIND OF VILLAINY** who convinced me to steal that wretched trophy."

Accomplice? OK, now my mind is racing.
Stefano isn't even the real bad guy. He's just
being used by the **ACTUAL THIEF**.

He faces us again. "We are simply doing what
needs to be done," he says, stomping his feet.
(Very unmysterious.)

"Stefano, I get that you're upset but you
shouldn't punish the whole town,"
Margaret Chow chimes in.

"If I can't have a cool
superpower, then nobody
can. It's not fair," he moans.
He reminds me of a big baby.

Maybe I should try a different
approach. *Think, Sara.*

I soften my voice and say, "Stefano.
Take it from me, as the only person here
without powers, you don't need special abilities
to be special. Look at Georgie. She's amazing
at football. Margaret is probably the smartest

student in our year and Javier speaks Spanish."

Stefano stares at me and I can see his mind racing. I continue.

"My dad always says that the most important thing is what you do for other people, not what you do yourself. That's what makes you a **TRUE HERO**."

I'm shocked when Stefano puffs out his chest and stands up straight. He starts tapping his chin with his finger. No way – he's actually falling for it.

"That makes sense, I guess." He looks around sheepishly. "I have been pretty selfish, huh?"

Yes! I scream in my head. I'm sure this is it. I feel I'm getting through to him. "You think we could have that trophy now? We'd all feel much happier when it's back safe and sound."

Georgie's gonna be so pleased! I have to force my face not to look too excited.

Eventually he agrees. "Yes. You know what, let me just grab it. I'll be back in a minute."

He slowly makes his way out, his

bodyguards following, looking baffled by the whole situation.

Margaret and Javier are grinning. We've done it. We've finally done it. Man, that was easy.

Maybe a little too easy.

Wait.

Pause.

Did that seem too easy?

Think about it. The reason there's all these plagues is because the trophy's **NOT IN WALSHAM**. That means he can't be back in a minute. Which means he's lying about grabbing the trophy.

Drats.

I jerk my head up just in time to see Stefano slam the classroom door shut. I sprint over, hopping over desks and chairs. But I hear the jingle of keys and the click of the door being locked.

SLAM!

158

"Noooo!" I shout. But it's too late. I hear his stupid laugh as Stefano walks away.

"MUHAHAHA. MUHAHAHA."

Ugh, even his laugh is irritating. He's the kind of guy who sits on the TV remote and accidentally changes the channel.

I grab the door handle, pulling and pulling with all my strength. Margaret Chow and Javier start screaming for help. We check our phones but there's no reception. We're trapped. **SUPER-DUPER TRAPPED**. And the football match has just started.

CHAPTER 12

LANGUAGES

Javier and Margaret Chow are **POUNDING** on the door. There has to be a way out. I tell them to stop shouting – I need to think.

Maybe opening locked doors is my power. I tell the others to step back and I place both my palms on the handle. I tense up, vibrating my whole body. Nothing happens. I shout, "Jamiroquai! Las-ketchup! Katchunchunga!" Nothing happens.

I take a step back. If I hold my hands up, maybe I can **BLAST IT OPEN**. I tense my jaw, squeezing my muscles, concentrating so hard I'm gonna burst. Instead, a squeaky fart escapes from my butt.

Javier whispers to Margaret, "Did she just let one rip?"

Sigh. At least it wasn't colourful. After all this, it would be so tragic if that was my ability.

"Guys, there are three of us. Let's put our heads together," I tell them. I look around. The window!

We race over to see if we can call out but – argh! – the windows are locked. We try prising them open but none of us are strong enough. The playground is empty anyway – the whole school must be at the football game.

We do have a good view of the road though. There's a lady walking her dog just outside the gates, but we're too far away.

Margaret Chow steps forward confidently. "I got this. Take cover. I'm going to use my power," she says with her chest out. **WOO!** Me and Javier cheer her on. "OK, Margaret, this is your time to shine," she tells herself. She brings two fingers up to her temple. She breathes in sharply. Her pupils disappear for a sec, like she's in a trance. Then her hand drops limply by her side, and she comes to.

"What happened?" Javier asks.

"That poodle down the road – he's feeling very regretful for being a bad dog. A very bad dog. Why did you have to do that on my side of the bed?" she says.

We stare at her. *What the smelly crumbs was that?*

"Sorry, sometimes my mind connects with the dog a little too much."

The lady with the dog disappears round the corner, and Javier sinks to the floor.

I hear my phone ping. We must have stepped

into a spot that has reception. It's a
voicemail from Georgie, sent just before the
game. I put it on speaker so the others can hear.

"Sara, where are you guys? Ramsdale's team
have just turned up so the match is starting soon.
Let me know what Stefano—" and that's where it
cuts off.

I try calling her back but the reception's
terrible. I listen to the voicemail again. And again.
Something doesn't feel right.

I look back out of the window. I watch as a fly
goes past. And, OMG, a thought goes straight
through my head.

Holy papadovski. No way.

It's like I've had amnesia this whole time and
I just forgot about it.

"Sara? You OK?" Margaret asks.

I'm more than OK. I'm terrified but I reckon
I've cracked it. Thinking out loud, I start at the
beginning, pacing round the room.

"The trophy cabinet. No fingerprints

or footprints. No signs of human tampering at all. That's because there *was* no human. Well, maybe he quickly became human, smashed the cabinet and immediately changed back."

I snap out of my trance. The clouds are getting darker by the minute. "Margaret, what do you know about Jock?"

She thinks for a sec. " Let me see. I know that the entire time he played for Ramsdale, they never won a match. He's the only one who didn't seem surprised by the rain that day it started.

Oh, and I know that his superpower, if you can call it that, is to turn into a fly. Other than that, Jock Isaacs is a mystery." She raises her eyebrow. "Sara? Why are you looking at me like that?"

My mouth is hanging wide open. No way. I'm super **EXCITED** but super **SHOOK UP** at the same time. I think back in my mind. It all makes sense!

I run over and quickly rummage through my bag, pulling out my copy of *The History of* WALSHAM TREASURE, and I check the

author. *Chloe Isaacs*. My stomach drops. My fears are confirmed.

I know someone else with that surname.

Someone who was there that day in the IT room with Kay.

Someone who was at football training the day it started raining.

Someone who was at the town library the first time we met Stefano.

Someone who transferred to our school from Ramsdale.

Someone who wants Walsham to lose their lucky trophy so his old school can finally win a football match.

Someone who has a grudge against Georgie, after she was voted in as team captain instead of him.

It's Jock Isaacs, and right now he's at the game with my best friend.

I explain about Jock to Javier and Margaret. I've got all these butterflies in my stomach. I have to get to that game. I have to warn Georgie. How did I miss all those signs?

It was a fly that made Kay sneeze and turn off all the computers.

There was a fly in the town library, **BUZZING** round the librarian as she was checking out our book.

The trophy cabinet door was broken from the inside. He must've got in as a fly and **SMASHED** his way out.

I was so convinced that Stefano had the trophy, but Jock Isaacs is the real culprit. He's the **VILLAIN** behind all this.

OK, Sara, it's now or never.

I go over to the window overlooking the playground and reach out my hand. *Come on, power, it's time to activate.* Nothing.

I puff out my cheeks. I stand on my head.

I do a funky-chicken dance. I say, "Cha-cha-cha!" in a baby voice, but nothing happens.

Behind me, Javier is working hard to unlock the classroom door. I guess that, after today, I'll never know what his power is. Poor Javier. Poor Margaret. Poor Georgie, my best friend in the world. Football means so much to her. And for everyone in this school, this town – the trophy is a part of who we are. I can't give up.

I'm concentrating on our playground, trying not to panic, and I close my eyes tight. Suddenly there's a cold gust of wind on my face.

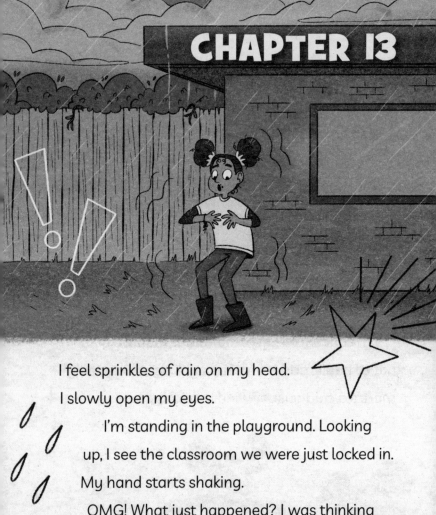

CHAPTER 13

I feel sprinkles of rain on my head.
I slowly open my eyes.

I'm standing in the playground. Looking
up, I see the classroom we were just locked in.
My hand starts shaking.

OMG! What just happened? I was thinking
about Jock being my nemesis. I was thinking
about saving Georgie. I was gazing out at the
playground, and I closed my eyes...

My hands are shaking, and my knees are
wobbly. I look over to the other side of the

playground by the school gates. I close my eyes and feel another **WHOOSH**! When I open them, I'm standing right in the place I was just looking at.

Woo! Yes! Funky-chicken celebration dance!

"Sara, what's going on?" Javier and Margaret Chow are running over. "One minute you were standing at the window, and when we looked up you weren't there any more," Margaret says, a little out of breath.

"I just teleported." I grin. "Javier, I did it. My power finally came through!" I shut my eyes, do the **WHOOSH!** thing and appear directly behind him. "Hi."

He screams and crouches with his hands over his head. Even Margaret has to do a little hop backwards, and I can tell she's impressed.

"How did you guys escape?" I'm still beaming at them.

Javier points at Margaret Chow who blushes and smiles. "That dog that I saw, I made a connection with it, like, in my mind, and I told it

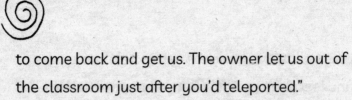

to come back and get us. The owner let us out of the classroom just after you'd teleported."

"Right. Well, that's pretty awesome."

I can tell she's really proud of herself, so I reach out and pat her on the head. Javier looks like he wants a pat on the head too – I can see it in his eyes – but there's no time!

"So, what's the plan?" Margaret asks urgently.

"We need to get to that football game, find Jock and figure out where he put the trophy."

They both nod in agreement, and Margaret Chow has got her serious face on. She's frowning slightly and tenses her jaw. We got this.

We race out of the gates towards the football ground. But when we get to the end of the road we're already out of breath. There's a clap of **THUNDER** that makes Javier scream and duck. It's actually quite scary, like a giant taking a photo with the flash on.

This is impossible – we don't have enough time.

"You could use your **TELEPORTATION** to get

there?" Javier suggests.

"That's not how it works." I picture how I did it before. "I think I need to see where I'm going," I tell him.

Another **LIGHTNING FORK** streaks across the clouds, and we all look up. I picture my mum in the clouds, **WHIZZING** around. That gives me an idea.

"Guys, I'm gonna teleport upwards." I point to the sky. "I might be able to see the football pitch from up there and teleport back down to it."

Margaret grabs my hand. "You can't – that's so dangerous," she says.

"I don't have a choice. Georgie could lose that game, the town could lose their powers, and there'll be no more IPA if we don't get that trophy back where it belongs."

"You're right." Javier nods. "I would come with you, but I've never done it in weather like this."

I don't know what he means but there's no time to ask.

His lip does a little wobble, like jelly on a plate. "I'm scared, Sara." Then he throws his arms round me in a little bear hug. Margaret joins in and whispers for me to be careful.

I squeeze them, then I find a space. I put my hands on my hips, **SUPERHERO POSE**, and look up to the clouds. *For Georgie*. I close my eyes tight.

Before I can even open them, I feel the ground underneath me disappear. I went from standing on the ground to not standing on anything.

For one split second, I'm the right way up. It's just me and the sky. But then...

I start falling through the air. Dropping faster and faster like a stone. I'm blinking cloud fog out of my eyes, and the wind is deafening, whistling in my ears.

I adjust myself so I'm flat on my stomach like a skydiver, just one without a parachute. No biggie. Hurtling to the ground, I can see the top

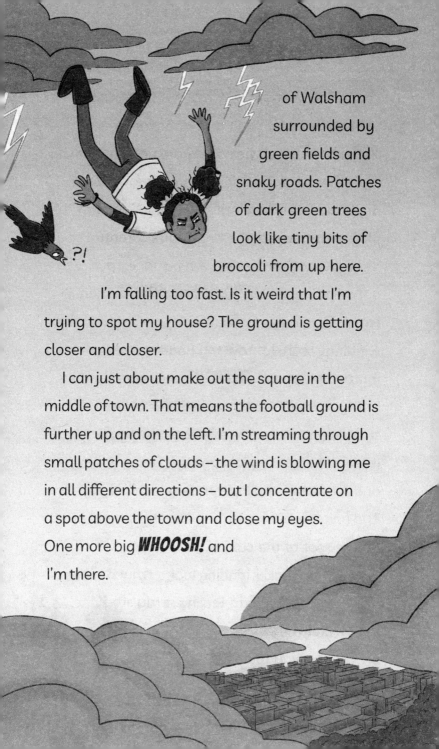

of Walsham
surrounded by
green fields and
snaky roads. Patches
of dark green trees
look like tiny bits of
broccoli from up here.

I'm falling too fast. Is it weird that I'm
trying to spot my house? The ground is getting
closer and closer.

I can just about make out the square in the
middle of town. That means the football ground is
further up and on the left. I'm streaming through
small patches of clouds – the wind is blowing me
in all different directions – but I concentrate on
a spot above the town and close my eyes.
One more big **WHOOSH!** and
I'm there.

This time I'm above a field with stands.

I push my body in that direction like a **DART**. The closer I get, the more I can see of the stands around the edge of the pitch – they're full of people. There are tiny dots of colour playing a game in the bright green centre.

Hold on, Georgie, I'm coming.

I'm falling, falling, falling, and then, when I'm close enough to see the tops of cars on the winding roads, I throw my head towards the football pitch and **TELEPORT** one more time.

My stomach does this little lurch. I'm suddenly standing on solid ground again. It feels like when you're in a lift going down, and it reaches the bottom floor too quickly. The only problem with my landing ... I end up on the roof of the stands.

My mum makes landing look so much cooler. I fall over immediately, feeling really **DIZZY**. Still, there'll be time for practice later. Hopefully.

I look around. There's loads of abandoned balls and frisbees up here, and I'm surrounded by murky puddles. *Yuk*. Below me, I can hear crowds cheering the football game. I carefully look over the edge of the roof at the pitch. Mr Ed Herring is blowing the whistle to signal half-time.

This is my opportunity.

As the players make their way towards the tunnel, the big scoreboard reads 7–0 to Ramsdale. Apparently Jock scored three own goals. The **TRAITOR**. I concentrate on the middle of the football pitch and, in one quick blink, I land in a superhero pose in front of everyone. True **BOSS MOVE** out here. *Whoop, whoop*. I grin. I start doing the funky-chicken dance.

"Stop it, Sara, we don't have time," I tell myself, and race down the tunnel.

I get a bit lost inside. I hear chatting coming from one of the changing rooms, so I kick the door open and jump in, screaming, "Aha! We have you now, Jock Isaacs! You thought you'd get

175

away with it, didn't you? Well, mark my words, it ends here. You're not messing with my town, my friends or my school ever again!"

The players around the changing room all fall silent. They stare up at me with their mouths open. "Jock Isaacs doesn't play for us any more," someone says. "I think you've got the wrong changing room."

Oh. Well, that's embarrassing. I quietly apologise and back out of the room. Across the way there's another door. I take a little run-up and **CRASH** through it.

"Aha!" I shout.

It's the cleaner's office. He has a mouthful of coffee and he spits it out everywhere. I look around and see a broom and keys on the wall, and a tiny desk and chair. OK, wrong room again.

As I close the door, I can hear him mutter to himself, "Only twelve weeks to retirement, Kev."

By the time I find our school's changing room, I don't even feel like bursting in. I'm sweaty and my legs hurt from all this running around. The moment's gone. I give the door a little knock. Big sigh of relief when Georgie opens it. She sees me standing there, shrieks with delight and gives me a giant hug.

I tell her under my breath that we found the **CULPRIT**.

"Oh," she whispers. "Who was it?"

Javier and Margaret come racing round the corner, and we all pile into the locker room. I ask them and Georgie to guard the door in case our suspect tries to escape, and we go in to confront him.

I walk to the centre of the changing room where the team are getting their boots on for the second half. "Not so fast, everyone."

Jock is staring up at me. There's no emotion on his face.

"You know why I'm here," I tell him. The rest of the team fall silent and turn to face him. "We know you used to play for Ramsdale, a team that hasn't beaten us in over eighty years. And when your relative, Chloe Isaacs, wrote that book about Valkro's treasure, you realised that our lucky trophy was in fact Valkro's treasure. You saw an opportunity, didn't you? So, you stole it and hid it outside town, knowing that it's our lucky trophy, because that's the only way Ramsdale could beat us. And you didn't care that we'd all lose our powers."

The whole changing room **GASPS**. Jock doesn't move, doesn't react.

"Where is it, Jock? Where did you hide it? This ends now," I continue.

A horrible smile appears on his face as he does a **SLOW CLAP**.

Kids who do a slow clap will probably grow into adults who jog on the spot at traffic lights.

"Well done, Sara. It took you long enough. You really wanna know where it is?" he says. "It's in my **SECRET TREE HOUSE**, at my family's holiday home near Norwich, *waaaaaaay* out of town."

He spends his holidays in Norwich?
No wonder he's a **SUPERVILLAIN**. "You'll
never find it," he continues, "and in an hour
it won't even matter. You've lost."

CHAPTER 14

RAMSDALE PRIMARY   WALSHAM PRIMARY

7   0

Jock Isaacs is the WORST. He's so smug. Georgie takes one tiny sniff and confirms that he's not lying about the tree house. The worst part is that we'll never find it in time. I clench my fists.

"Was it worth it?" I ask. "All these plagues? You're gonna mess everything up, and for what? For one football match?"

I'm standing right in front of him. He's got nowhere to run. He just does this horrible grin, showing all his teeth. "You think this is all about one football match?" His smirk turns into a frown.

"This is for eighty years of football games. All those losses, all that **HEARTBREAK**, and all because of that stupid trophy." Now I can see the anger in his eyes.

Over in the corner, I clock Margaret and Javier checking something on their phones.

Jock stands up. The corners of his mouth are frothing when he talks. "You know how my aunt Chloe knew so much about Valkro Strapp? How she knew such heavily guarded **FAMILY SECRETS**?"

I know what he's gonna say before he says it. No way.

"We're his direct descendants. And what did we get for it? Nothing. Nobody in my family ever joined the **IPA**, ever won a football match, ever became anything. It's not fair. My bloodline gave this town its powers, and I'm the one who's gonna take them away." A big flash of **LIGHTNING** lights him up from behind.

Someone taps me on the shoulder. It's Margaret Chow. "Sara, you might want to see this," she says in my ear.

"Not now. We're kinda in the middle of something," I tell her.

"Sara, I really think you should look at this." She holds out her phone. If this is a meme, I'm gonna be so upset.

It's a picture of Jock with the trophy. She found it on his blog, posted a few hours before the game. He must have thought it was too late for anyone to stop him. I don't get why she's showing me. We'll never find it.

"*Look* at *where* the picture was taken," she says, but it's just in a stupid tree house.

"Erm, hello?" Jock says.

I ignore him. I finally twig why Margaret's showing me this.

I can only teleport to places I can see. I look at the picture on her phone, concentrating on the place rather than the treasure.

I close my eyes and **WHOOSH!**

I open them, and I'm there in the empty tree house. I can smell dusty old wood. It's a little cold in here.

My stomach does a little **BACKFLIP** when I spot something glinting in the corner. I feel my phone vibrate in my pocket, a message from Javier. There's no words. It's just a photo of the changing room, with everyone still in it.

My heart does a big jump; my whole body is shaking with excitement like I've just been **ZAPPED** by Kay.

Seriously, I love my friends.

I grab the football trophy, concentrate on the picture Javier just sent and **TELEPORT** straight back.

Jock's mouth falls open when he sees me standing there with the trophy. The other players on the team start clapping and **CHEERING**. Georgie and Javier grab me in a group hug, while Margaret Chow stands there, looking sheepish. I pull her into our hug too.

183

Jock starts screaming, "No, no, this can't be!"

I make my way over to him. "Face it, Jock, you're a joke," I tell him. Javier giggles, and I'm grinning too. (That joke was hilarious-ish.)

Jock stands there and points his finger at me. "This isn't the last you'll see of me, Sara. Everywhere you look, I will always be there to foil your plans. You'll never get rid of me! Until we meet again!"

He swishes his arm around and ... turns into a little fly.

He starts to make his escape, buzzing towards the tiny window on the far wall. It looks like he's

about to make a smooth getaway but
when he gets to the window...

Bump.
Ping.
Bounce.
Bump.

Fly-Jock just keeps hitting the window.
Over and over again. We're all staring at him.
Someone coughs.

In the end, Georgie opens the window a little
wider, and Jock finally escapes. Javier is holding a
fly swatter that he quietly puts back in his pocket.

We all fall silent when Jock has gone. I'm
speechless. Georgie puts her hand on my
shoulder. Before I can help it, I'm suddenly
jumping for joy.

"**YES!**" I'm punching the air in celebration. Javier
congratulates me for finishing our investigation.

"That's not why I'm celebrating," I tell him.

I have the biggest smile on my face.

"It isn't?"

"Nope. Do you realise what just happened? I have a **NEMESIS**!"

From now on, I'm looking at endless **CLASHES** with Jock Isaacs, **BATTLES** to fight, **CASES** to solve, plans to **THWART**. I just got one step closer to being a proper hero and joining the **IPA**.

I load up a picture of the school hallway and trophy cabinet on my phone (and hope that one day I'll be able to teleport to places without having to look at them).

I land in the quiet corridor and make my way over to the broken cabinet. As I get closer, I can almost feel the trophy in my hands pulling me forward. Almost like it wants to go home.

I slowly place it back in its spot. A tiny **SHIMMER** flashes across the surface. Outside, the clouds part immediately. Sunlight comes pouring through the window, and I smile to myself. I missed the blue skies.

I take a step back
and salute the trophy.
We need to make sure
it's protected from
now on.

I open my phone
gallery and teleport
back to the football ground.

The rest of the afternoon feels like a blur.
Javier's next to me in the stands. He has no idea
what's happening in the game, he's just happy
sunbathing for the first time in days.
We've decided not to go after Stefano,
not yet, but just to enjoy the match.

Because Jock turned into a fly and left,
Margaret Chow had to take his place on the
football pitch. She gets a super-loud cheer from
her friends when she comes on. Georgie's been

on fire – scoring four goals and assisting three more. In the last minute of the game, she glides past three Ramsdale players, nutmegs another and crosses the ball with her left foot. The ball hits Margaret Chow's head, loops over the goalkeeper and rolls into the back of the net. Final score: 8–7.

The team hoist Margaret on to their shoulders and give her a lap of honour round the pitch.

Ramsdale Primary	Walsham Primary
7	8

She screams happily, waving her hands in the air as she passes us. Javier waves back, and blushes when he notices me looking.

In the far corner of the pitch, Georgie's parents are there, both suited and booted. Her dad reaches out to shake her hand but she grabs both of them in a giant hug. She deserves that.

The Ramsdale players start trudging back to their locker room, but Georgie runs over to stop them. "Do you guys wanna stick around? We can play a friendly game, mix up the teams a little?" she asks Lilly, their captain.

I can see the shock on her face but then she just nods and smiles.

Georgie comes running over to the stands. "Sara! Javier!" she calls. "You guys are with me. We're shooting that way."

Javier puts his headphones on and tells her he can't hear. He deserves a rest.

I start making my way down to the pitch but I spot something on the opposite side of the field. My dad, standing in his **SUPERHERO POSE**, and my mum, **GLIDING** over to join him, landing in hers. My parents are so cool. Even from here, I can see that they're a little out of breath, but there's a smile on both their faces. Mum's hair is all messy and blown about, and Dad's superhero costume is torn in several places.

I barely have to blink and **WHOOSH!** I land right in my mum's arms. I don't care that her clothes are a bit damp. I wrap my arms around her. Then Dad picks both of us up in a great big bear hug.

"Well done, munchkin," he says.

"We're so proud of you," Mum whispers.

"You guys were right," I tell them. "I did that whole investigation without my powers."

My friends helped me, of course. Georgie, the **HUMAN LIE DETECTOR**, Margaret Chow, the **DOG WHISPERER**, and Javier, the – **WAIT**, where did he go? From here, I can see his seat in the stands is empty. We never did find out what his power is.

But it's not our superpowers that make us **SPECIAL**.

Being a real superhero isn't about the powers we have, it's about the things we do to help others. And wherever we're needed next, powers or no powers, me and my friends will be there.